VOODOO

A Southern Gothic Horror

ARIEL SANDERS

Copyright © 2025 by ARIEL SANDERS
All rights reserved.

No part of this book may be reproduced, stored in a retrieval system, or transmitted in any form or by any means—electronic, mechanical, photocopying, recording, or otherwise—without the prior written permission of the publisher, except in the case of brief quotations used in reviews.

This book is intended for entertainment purposes only. While every effort has been made to ensure accuracy, the author and publisher make no representations or warranties regarding the completeness, accuracy, or reliability of the information contained within. The reader assumes full responsibility for their interpretation and application of any content in this book.

Index

Chapter 1 The Return	5
Chapter 2 The Inheritance	21
Chapter 3 The Marked	39
Chapter 4 The Binding	65
Chapter 5 The Rite of Seven	81
Epilogue Ashes and Salt	89

SPECIAL BONUS

Want this Bonus Ebook for *free*?

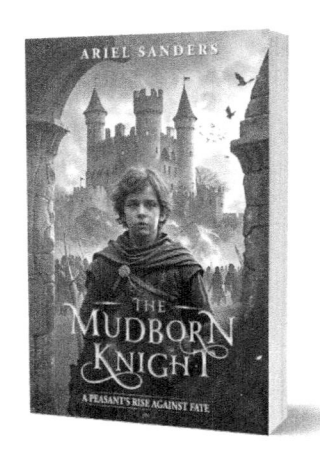

SCAN W/ YOUR CAMERA TO DOWNLOAD THE EBOOK!

Chapter 1
The Return

The air in Belle Noire hung thick with moisture and memory. Camille DuPont stepped off the ancient bus that had rattled its way from New Orleans, her designer boots sinking slightly into the soft ground. The journey from New York had stripped away her urban armor—first the flight delays, then the rental car breaking down just outside of Baton Rouge, forcing her onto this local bus that smelled of tobacco and regret.

She stood alone at the unmarked stop, a slender figure in black against the verdant overgrowth of the Louisiana bayou. Heat pressed against her skin like an unwelcome embrace. How strange to think that for the first eighteen years of her life, this suffocating warmth had been as natural as breathing.

"You came back after all, Miss Camille."

The voice startled her. An elderly man with skin like cracked leather emerged from the shade of a massive live oak. Mr. Thibodeaux—she recognized him from childhood, though the years had bent his once-imposing frame.

"I didn't have much choice," she replied, hefting her single suitcase. "Grandmère made sure of that."

"Mmm." The old man nodded, eyes narrowing slightly. "Marie-Claire DuPont never did anything without purpose, even dying."

Camille felt a chill despite the heat. "So you heard."

"Everybody heard, chère. Your grandmother was Belle Noire's oldest daughter." He gestured to a rusted pickup truck. "Need a ride to Le Vert?"

She hesitated only a moment before climbing in. The truck smelled of fish and gasoline, but Camille was beyond caring. Forty-eight hours of travel had left her numb.

"When did you get the letter?" Mr. Thibodeaux asked as the truck lurched forward down the narrow parish road.

Camille's hand instinctively went to her jacket pocket, where the cream-colored envelope rested like a talisman. "Three days ago. Just hours after she—" The words stuck in her throat.

Three days ago, she'd been reviewing copy for the magazine's summer issue when the courier arrived. The international delivery had seemed out of place among the sleek electronics and modern furnishings of her Manhattan office. The wax seal bearing the fleur-de-lis had immediately transported her back to childhood summers spent watching her grandmother press that same insignia into melted burgundy wax.

"I know what the letter says," Mr. Thibodeaux offered, his eyes fixed on the road ahead. "She told me what she wrote to you."

Camille pulled out the envelope, brittle now from how many times she had unfolded and refolded its contents.

My dearest Camille,

If you are reading this, I have passed beyond the veil. Do not grieve overlong—death comes to us all, and at ninety-two, I have cheated him longer than most.

You must return to Belle Noire immediately. The protection I have maintained is failing. The unfinished rites must be completed, or what sleeps beneath Le Vert will awaken fully. The bloodline calls to its own.

There is a room you were forbidden to enter as a child. The key hangs around my neck as I write this. By the time you read these words, it will be with my body in the earth. You must retrieve it.

Time grows short. The signs are appearing. Already I see shadows where none should be.

Return home, granddaughter. The DuPont legacy awaits its final keeper.

—*Grandmère*

Camille had read it a dozen times, searching for some hidden meaning, some explanation that would make sense of the cryptic warnings. Journalist that she was, she'd researched "unfinished rites" and "bloodline protection," finding only vague references to voodoo practices and Creole superstitions.

"She was sick a long time," Camille said finally. "Dementia, perhaps?"

Mr. Thibodeaux's laugh was dry and humorless. "Your grandmother's mind was sharp as a gator's tooth till the end. No, what ailed Marie-Claire wasn't of the mind."

The truck rounded a bend, and suddenly the road opened up to reveal Belle Noire proper. Camille's breath caught. The town seemed frozen in time—weathered clapboard buildings lined the single main street, their paint peeling in the humid air. A handful of locals moved languidly through daily routines that seemed unchanged from decades past. The modern world had barely touched this place.

"We're having the service tonight," Mr. Thibodeaux said, turning onto a narrow side street. "Sunset burial, like she wanted."

"Tonight?" Camille frowned. "But I just arrived. Surely we can wait until—"

"Can't wait," he interrupted firmly. "Been three days already. In this heat..." He trailed off meaningfully.

The realization that her grandmother's body had been kept unburied for three days sent another chill through Camille. "Why wait for me at all?"

"She was specific. Said the blood must be present for the passing."

They drove in silence past the town limits, following a winding dirt road that cut through dense cypress groves. Spanish moss hung like spectral curtains, filtering the afternoon sunlight into strange, shifting patterns. After fifteen minutes, the trees gave way to reveal Le Vert Manor in the distance.

The plantation house stood on a slight rise, its once-white columns now gray with age and neglect. Two stories of crumbling grandeur surrounded by creeping vegetation, windows like vacant eyes staring out over the surrounding swampland. Behind it, barely visible, was the small family cemetery enclosed by a rusted wrought-iron fence.

As they approached, Camille noticed figures moving around the property—townspeople preparing for the funeral, she assumed. The truck pulled up to the front steps, and she stepped out, feeling strangely like a stranger at what had once been her childhood home.

"You remember the way to your room?" Mr. Thibodeaux asked, not offering to carry her bag.

"Yes, thank you." Camille hesitated. "Will you stay for the—"

"I'll be back at sunset," he said, already turning the truck around. "Best get yourself settled. It's going to be a long night."

Camille watched him drive away before facing the house again. The front door stood open, as if expecting her. With a deep breath, she climbed the steps, the wood creaking beneath her weight.

The foyer was exactly as she remembered—ornate ceiling medallion, curved staircase, faded portraits of DuPont ancestors lining the walls. The only difference was the scent—beneath the familiar smell of old wood and beeswax polish was something earthy and pungent. Herbs, perhaps, or incense.

"Hello?" she called, setting down her suitcase. "Is anyone here?"

Movement from the parlor drew her attention. A tall woman emerged, dressed in a simple black dress that contrasted sharply with the colorful scarf wrapped around her head. Eloise Laveau, her grandmother's housekeeper for as long as Camille could remember.

"Miss Camille," Eloise said, her face betraying no emotion. "You've arrived."

"Eloise." Camille stepped forward to embrace the woman, but stopped when Eloise made no move to reciprocate. Instead, the housekeeper gave a slight nod.

"Your room is prepared. The funeral begins at sunset."

"Thank you," Camille said, suddenly awkward. "I was surprised to hear the burial was scheduled so quickly."

"Madame's wishes were very specific." Eloise glanced toward the staircase. "You should rest before the ceremony. It will be... demanding."

Before Camille could ask what she meant, another voice called from deeper in the house.

"Is that her? Is she here?" An elderly woman Camille didn't recognize appeared in the doorway to the dining room, her rheumy eyes wide with curiosity or fear—Camille couldn't tell which.

"Yes, Madame Broussard. The granddaughter has returned," Eloise answered.

The old woman made a gesture that Camille recognized vaguely as a protective sign against evil—thumb tucked between middle and ring fingers, a subtle movement but deliberate.

"Does she know?" Madame Broussard asked Eloise, speaking as if Camille weren't present.

"Not yet," Eloise replied softly. "There will be time after."

Camille felt her journalistic instincts sharpen through the haze of grief and exhaustion. "Know what? What's going on here?"

Eloise turned back to her, expression carefully neutral. "Your grandmother's passing has been difficult for the town. She was... important to many people."

"More than you know, girl," Madame Broussard muttered, retreating back into the dining room.

Camille stood there, absorbing the strangeness of her welcome. Finally, she picked up her suitcase. "I'll go freshen up before the service."

"I've laid out appropriate clothes," Eloise said. "And Miss Camille?" Her voice softened slightly. "Welcome home."

The stairs creaked under Camille's weight as she climbed to the second floor. The hallway stretched before her, lined with closed doors—guest rooms mostly, though at the far end was her grandmother's suite. Her own childhood room was halfway down on the right.

The door stuck slightly before giving way. Inside, time seemed to have stopped. The same flowered wallpaper, now faded and peeling in places. The same four-poster bed with its hand-stitched quilt. Even her old school pennant still hung above the desk.

On the bed lay a simple black dress—not hers, but clearly laid out for the funeral. Beside it was a small leather-bound book that Camille recognized immediately as her grandmother's journal.

Frowning, she picked it up. The journal had been her grandmother's constant companion, always kept locked and private. Why would it be here now?

She opened it to find a pressed flower marking a page. Her grandmother's elegant script filled the margins around what appeared to be a ritual of some kind. Words in a mixture of French and what might have been Haitian Creole surrounded a carefully drawn symbol—a vevé, Camille realized, remembering fragments of her childhood education about local traditions.

The Binding must hold until she returns. Baron Samedi grows impatient, but I have given enough blood to satisfy him for now. The seventh veil remains intact.

Camille flipped through more pages, finding similar cryptic entries alongside pressed flowers, feathers, and what looked disturbingly like locks of human hair pressed between the pages. Dates jumped backward and forward—her grandmother had not kept the journal chronologically but seemed to revisit and add to entries over decades.

A loose photograph slipped from between the pages. Camille picked it up, recognizing her eight-year-old self standing beside her grandmother in the backyard. They were beside the old well, and her grandmother was in the middle of drawing something in the dirt with a stick. The little girl—Camille—looked solemn, almost afraid.

She turned the photo over. Written in her grandmother's hand: *First binding, 1997. She doesn't understand yet. Better that way.*

Something scratched at the window, startling her. A branch from the magnolia tree outside, swaying in a sudden breeze. Camille set the journal down and moved to the window, looking out over the property.

People were gathering now, townsfolk dressed in black making their way toward the family cemetery. Some carried instruments—a violin, an accordion, a small drum. Others held candles despite the daylight. And standing apart from them all, at the edge of the swamp that bordered the property, was a lone figure in white.

Camille squinted, trying to make out details, but the figure was too distant. As she watched, it seemed to raise a hand toward her—a greeting? A warning?—before turning and disappearing into the treeline.

A knock at the door made her jump.

"Miss Camille?" Eloise's voice. "It's nearly time."

"I'll be right down," she called back, her eyes still searching the spot where the figure had vanished.

She changed quickly into the black dress, which fit as if made for her. As she slipped on the accompanying black lace shawl, she noticed something tucked into its folds—a small cloth doll, crudely made but achingly familiar.

Camille's breath caught. It was her childhood doll, the one her grandmother had made for her sixth birthday. She'd called it her "guardian angel," a constant companion until she left for college. She'd assumed it lost years ago.

"Why now?" she whispered, turning the doll over in her hands. Small stitches formed X's where the eyes should be, and around its neck was a tiny red thread tied in an intricate knot.

The doll had always been a comfort, but now it felt like a message—or a warning. Impulsively, she tucked it into the pocket of her dress before heading downstairs.

The funeral procession was already forming in the front yard. Eloise waited at the bottom of the stairs, holding a small bundle of white flowers.

"For your grandmother," she explained, handing them to Camille. "You'll need to lead us to the grave."

Outside, the gathering had grown. At least thirty people stood in loose formation, many faces Camille vaguely recognized from childhood. They parted silently as she emerged from the house, their expressions solemn but watchful.

The coffin sat on a simple wooden cart at the bottom of the steps. It was made of dark cypress wood and, Camille noticed with a start, was covered in symbols—some carved directly into the wood, others painted in white. At the center of the lid was a vevé that matched the one in her grandmother's journal.

"What are these?" she asked Eloise quietly.

"Protection," came the simple reply. "And passage."

Mr. Thibodeaux and three other men stepped forward to take positions at each corner of the cart. They nodded to Camille, waiting.

Unsure of what was expected, she placed her flowers on the coffin and moved to the front of the cart. A murmur of approval rippled through the gathering.

"The blood leads," someone whispered behind her.

As if on cue, the musicians began to play—a slow, melancholy tune that Camille recognized from childhood funerals. The procession began to move, winding around the side of the house toward the family cemetery.

The sun hung low on the horizon now, casting long shadows across the grounds. As they walked, Camille became aware of soft chanting behind her, voices rising and falling in what sounded like a mixture of prayer and incantation. Words in French and Creole blended together, sometimes rising enough for her to catch phrases:

"Baron, guide her path... Seven veils between worlds... The blood must complete what blood began..."

The small cemetery came into view, its wrought iron gate standing open. Inside, fresh earth marked a new grave beside the weathered headstones of DuPont ancestors. Camille led the procession through the gate, feeling a strange vibration in the air as she crossed the threshold, as if passing through an invisible membrane.

The cart was positioned beside the open grave, and the coffin lifted carefully by the pallbearers. As they lowered it onto the straps positioned to ease it into the earth, Eloise stepped forward with a small clay jar.

"The offering," she announced, unscrewing the lid to reveal a dark, viscous liquid that smelled of rum and herbs.

Eloise dipped her fingers into the mixture and traced a symbol on the coffin lid—another vevé, different from the carved one. She then turned to Camille, holding out the jar.

"You must make the mark of passage," she instructed. "Your blood remembers the way."

Hesitantly, Camille dipped her fingers into the jar. The liquid was warm against her skin, almost alive. Without knowing why, her hand moved of its own accord, tracing a pattern she didn't consciously recognize yet somehow knew. A cross, then curved lines emanating outward like a spider's web.

As she completed the symbol, the last rays of sunlight disappeared below the horizon. In the sudden dimness, Camille could have sworn the mark briefly glowed before fading into the wood.

"Now the token," Eloise said, her voice taking on a rhythmic cadence. "The guardian must accompany the guardian."

Camille understood suddenly. She withdrew the cloth doll from her pocket, feeling strangely reluctant to part with it. "This was supposed to be buried with her?"

Eloise nodded. "It has watched over you. Now it must watch over her passage."

The gathered mourners had formed a circle around the grave, their faces ghostly in the gathering dusk. Someone lit lanterns, casting wavering shadows across the scene.

Camille placed the doll atop the coffin, next to the symbol she had drawn. As soon as she did, the chanting grew louder, more urgent. The musicians played faster, their melody transforming into something primal and unsettling.

"Lower her now," Eloise commanded, and the pallbearers began to work the straps, easing the coffin into the earth.

As it descended, Camille felt a sudden rush of dizziness. The world seemed to tilt sideways, colors bleeding into one another. For a moment—just a moment—she thought she saw something move within the grave, beneath the coffin. Something dark and sinuous, like smoke given form.

"Grandmère," she whispered, swaying slightly.

Strong hands steadied her—Eloise on one side, Mr. Thibodeaux on the other.

"It's beginning," Eloise murmured. "She feels it already."

"Feels what?" Camille asked, but her words were drowned out by a sudden gust of wind that swept through the cemetery, extinguishing half the lanterns.

In the new darkness, the first shovelful of earth hit the coffin with a hollow thud. Then another, and another. The musicians played on, now joined by the rhythmic beating of small drums produced from beneath mourners' coats.

As the grave filled, Camille noticed something strange. The cloth doll, which should have been buried with the first layer of dirt, somehow remained visible on top of the growing mound. Each shovelful seemed to miss it, or perhaps it was being deliberately uncovered.

When the grave was filled and patted down, the doll still sat atop the fresh earth, its stitched face turned upward toward the emerging stars.

Eloise bent down and retrieved it, then pressed it back into Camille's hands.

"It returns to you," she said. "The guardian has chosen."

"I don't understand," Camille replied, clutching the doll. "What does this mean?"

But Eloise had already turned away, speaking rapidly in Creole to the gathered mourners. They began to disperse, some making signs of protection as they passed Camille, others refusing to meet her eye.

Only Mr. Thibodeaux lingered, his weathered face grave in the lantern light.

"Your grandmother kept things at bay for many years," he said quietly. "Now that burden passes to you."

"What burden? What things?" Camille demanded, frustration breaking through her confusion. "Will someone please speak plainly?"

"There's a reason you left Belle Noire," he replied. "There's a reason your grandmother allowed it, even encouraged it. She was buying time."

"Time for what?"

"For you to grow strong enough to finish what she started." He nodded toward the house. "Eloise will explain. Tonight, you must rest. Tomorrow, your real work begins."

With that cryptic statement, he turned and followed the others, leaving Camille alone beside her grandmother's grave.

The night had fully descended now, the cemetery illuminated only by the few remaining lanterns and the thin crescent moon overhead. Camille stood frozen, the doll clutched in her hand, feeling as though she'd stepped into someone else's life— someone else's nightmare.

A soft noise from behind one of the larger headstones caught her attention. She peered into the darkness, seeing nothing at first. Then, movement—a small, dark shape darting between graves.

"Hello?" she called, her voice sounding unnaturally loud in the quiet cemetery. "Is someone there?"

No answer came, but as she watched, more shadows seemed to detach themselves from the darkness, moving with purpose around the perimeter of the cemetery. Not people—too small, too quick. Animals perhaps, though she couldn't identify what kind.

The wind picked up again, carrying with it whispered words too faint to make out. Camille backed away from the grave, suddenly eager to return to the relative safety of the house.

As she turned toward the gate, her foot struck something. Looking down, she saw a small object on the ground—a wooden medallion on a leather cord. She picked it up, holding it to the nearest lantern. Carved into its surface was a symbol similar to the one she'd traced on the coffin.

She slipped it over her head without knowing why, feeling somehow that it belonged with her. As the medallion settled against her skin, a strange warmth spread through her chest.

The cemetery gate creaked as she pushed through it, the sound unnaturally loud in the quiet night. Looking back one last time at her grandmother's grave, Camille froze.

A figure stood beside the fresh mound—a woman in white, her back to Camille. The same figure she'd seen at the edge of the swamp earlier?

"Excuse me," Camille called, taking a step back toward the grave. "Are you—"

The figure turned slowly. In the dim light, Camille could make out few details, but one thing was clear—where the woman's mouth should have been was only smooth, unbroken skin, as if it had been sewn shut and then healed over entirely.

Camille's breath caught in her throat. She blinked once, hard, and when she looked again, the figure was gone. Only the night breeze remained, stirring the Spanish moss that hung from the cemetery's ancient oak.

With her heart pounding, Camille hurried back toward Le Vert Manor, the cloth doll clutched tightly in one hand, the other pressed against the wooden medallion at her throat. Behind her, too faint to be certain, came the sound of soft laughter—or perhaps it was only the wind in the cypress trees.

Either way, as Camille climbed the steps to her ancestral home, she couldn't shake the feeling that something had awakened in Belle Noire. Something that had been waiting a very long time for her return.

Chapter 2
The Inheritance

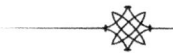

Morning came reluctantly to Le Vert Manor, gray light filtering through heavy curtains that Camille didn't remember closing. She lay still for several moments, orienting herself in the unfamiliar familiarity of her childhood bedroom. The events of the previous day—the strange funeral, the mysterious doll, the figure in the cemetery—seemed dreamlike in the wan daylight.

She reached for her phone on the bedside table. No service, as expected. Belle Noire existed in one of Louisiana's notorious dead zones. Her editor in New York would be wondering where her copy was for next week's issue. The thought of the real world—her world of deadlines and fact-checking and cocktail parties—seemed impossibly distant.

Something scratched against the floor. Camille sat up to find the cloth doll lying at the foot of her bed, though she was certain she'd placed it on the dresser before falling into exhausted sleep. A coincidence—it must have fallen and been kicked there when she turned in her sleep.

A soft knock at the door preceded Eloise's entrance. The housekeeper carried a tray with coffee and what smelled like fresh beignets.

"You slept well?" Eloise asked, setting the tray on a small table by the window.

"Well enough," Camille lied, pushing back the covers. The wooden medallion she'd found in the cemetery still hung around her neck. She touched it absently. "What time is it?"

"Nearly ten. The notary will be here at noon." Eloise pulled back the curtains, letting in more light. The day outside was overcast, threatening rain.

"Notary?"

"For the reading of the will." Eloise poured coffee into a delicate china cup that Camille recognized from childhood—her grandmother's best service, used only for important guests. "Your grandmother left everything in order."

Camille sipped the coffee—strong and sweet, with chicory, the way her grandmother always made it. "I'm not staying, Eloise. Whatever this is about, I have a life in New York. A career."

"You have obligations here now." Eloise's tone left no room for argument. "Blood obligations."

"I buried her. What more—"

"That was only the beginning." Eloise moved to the door, pausing with her hand on the knob. "Eat, dress. There is much to discuss before Mr. Fontenot arrives."

When Eloise had gone, Camille sat in the window seat, watching wispy tendrils of mist rise from the bayou beyond the property. In daylight, Le Vert Manor revealed more of its decay—peeling paint, sagging porch boards, shutters hanging askew. The family fortune had dwindled long ago, leaving only the land and the house as reminders of former glory.

After washing and dressing in the adjoining bathroom—plumbing modernized sometime in the seventies, with ancient pipes that groaned and sputtered—Camille made her way downstairs. The house seemed different in daylight, less threatening but more melancholy.

She found Eloise in the kitchen, grinding herbs with a mortar and pestle. The pungent smell from yesterday—part medicinal, part earthy—was stronger here.

"What is that?" Camille asked, leaning against the doorframe.

"Protection," Eloise replied without looking up. "The barriers are thinning."

"Barriers between what?"

Eloise set down the pestle and fixed Camille with a steady gaze. "Between the living and the dead. Between this world and the other."

Camille sighed. "Eloise, I respect that you and Grandmère shared certain... beliefs. But I'm not—"

"Not a believer. I know." Eloise resumed grinding. "Neither was your mother. That's why she ran, why she took you away. But belief is not required for truth to exist, Miss Camille."

The mention of her mother—dead these fifteen years from cancer—caught Camille off guard. "My mother left because she wanted a different life. Modern medicine, not..." She gestured at the herbs.

"Your mother left because she was afraid," Eloise corrected. "Afraid of what flows in her veins. In your veins."

Before Camille could respond, a knock at the front door echoed through the house. Eloise wiped her hands on her apron.

"Early," she muttered, heading for the foyer.

Curious, Camille followed. Through the etched glass panels flanking the front door, she could make out the silhouette of a man in a hat.

Eloise opened the door to reveal Mr. Thibodeaux, his expression grim. "There's been another one," he said without preamble.

"Where?" Eloise asked, her normally impassive face showing alarm.

"Breaux farm. Cattle again. Like the others."

"How many?"

"Three. All... like before."

Eloise pressed her lips into a thin line. "It's escalating. Show me."

She turned to Camille. "The notary comes at noon. Wait for him in the study. Do not leave the house."

Before Camille could protest, Eloise had grabbed a small bag from a hook by the door and followed Mr. Thibodeaux outside. Through the window, Camille watched them climb into his truck and drive away, dust billowing behind them.

Left alone in the vast house, Camille felt a prickle of unease. What had they been talking about? What was happening to cattle at the Breaux farm?

The journalist in her couldn't resist investigating. She found her grandmother's study easily—a room she remembered being forbidden from entering as a child. Unlike the rest of the house, it showed signs of recent use. Papers were stacked neatly on a mahogany desk. Bookshelves lined the walls, filled with ancient volumes in French, English, and languages Camille didn't recognize.

On the desk sat a leather folio marked "Testament et Dernières Volontés" in her grandmother's elegant script. The will, presumably. Beside it lay a ring of old iron keys, each labeled with faded paper tags.

Camille picked up the keys, examining the labels. "East Wing." "Wine Cellar." "Attic." And one, smaller than the rest, simply marked "B."

The basement. The letter had mentioned a room she was forbidden to enter as a child. Could this be the key?

A sound from elsewhere in the house made her start—a soft thud, as if something had fallen. She set down the keys and moved cautiously into the hallway.

"Hello? Is someone there?"

No answer came, but another sound followed—a scraping, like furniture being moved. It seemed to be coming from the parlor.

Camille approached slowly, aware of her heartbeat accelerating. The parlor door stood ajar, though she was certain it had been closed earlier.

"Eloise?" she called, knowing it was futile. She'd watched the housekeeper leave.

She pushed the door open wider. The parlor was empty, sunlight streaming through lace curtains to illuminate dust motes dancing in the air. Nothing seemed disturbed.

Until she looked at the portrait above the fireplace.

It had been there as long as she could remember—her great-great-grandmother, Josephine DuPont, seated primly in a high-backed chair, her expression severe. But now, the portrait hung crookedly, as if someone had jostled it.

Camille stepped closer, intending to straighten it. As she reached up, she noticed something behind the frame—a slight gap between the portrait and the wall, revealing what looked like paper.

Carefully, she lifted the heavy frame away from the wall. Behind it was an envelope, yellowed with age, secured to the back of the canvas. Her name was written across it in her grandmother's hand.

Heart pounding, Camille removed the envelope and opened it. Inside was a single sheet of paper, densely covered in her grandmother's script.

Camille,

If you are reading this, you have already begun to experience the awakening. The signs will be subtle at first—objects moved, shadows where none should be, whispers at the edge of hearing. These are the loa testing the boundaries, sensing the change in guardianship.

What you must understand: Our family has been bound to them for seven generations, since Josephine made the first pact in 1868. She sought power during Reconstruction, a way to preserve our way of life when all seemed lost. The loa gave her what she asked for, but at a price.

Seven generations, seven veils between worlds. Each DuPont daughter has maintained the barriers, kept the most dangerous entities at bay through ritual and sacrifice. I have held them longer than most, but my time is ending.

You are the seventh, Camille. The last. In you, the circle must either be completed or broken forever.

Trust Eloise. She is more than she appears. The Laveau line has guided ours since the beginning.

The basement room contains what you need to understand. The ritual tools, the names, the history of our burden. But be warned—to enter is to acknowledge your role. The loa will sense your acceptance and respond accordingly.

There is no middle path. You either take up the mantle or you break the pact entirely. Both choices carry terrible consequences.

Blood calls to blood, Camille. Listen carefully.

—Marie-Claire

Camille's hands trembled as she folded the letter and slipped it into her pocket. Seven generations? A pact with voodoo spirits? It sounded like madness, like the ramblings of an old woman lost in superstition and folklore.

And yet...

She thought of the strange funeral, the symbols on the coffin. The cloth doll that returned when it should have been buried. The figure in the cemetery with no mouth.

Outside, thunder rumbled—a storm approaching from the Gulf. The parlor darkened as clouds obscured the sun, casting the room into shadow. In that moment, Camille could have sworn she saw movement in the corner of her eye—a flicker of something dark and formless, there and gone too quickly to identify.

A loud knock at the front door made her jump. The notary, most likely.

Hurriedly, she rehung the portrait, straightening it on the wall. As she stepped back, she noticed something odd—Josephine's eyes in the painting seemed to follow her movement, though she was certain they had been gazing straight ahead before.

Another knock, more insistent. Camille shook off her unease and went to answer it.

Mr. Fontenot was exactly as she remembered him from childhood visits—rail-thin, with spectacles perched on a nose like a beak, and fingers permanently stained with ink. He carried a weathered leather briefcase and smelled faintly of tobacco and cologne.

"Miss DuPont," he greeted her, removing his hat. "My condolences on your loss. Your grandmother was a remarkable woman."

"Thank you," Camille replied, ushering him inside. "Eloise had to step out, but she said we should meet in the study."

"Yes, quite right. Legal matters, best handled formally." Mr. Fontenot followed her down the hallway, his shoes clicking on the hardwood floors. "Have you had a chance to review the preliminary documents?"

"No, I only arrived yesterday."

"Ah." He nodded understanding. "Well, Madame DuPont's wishes were quite explicit. The process should be straightforward."

In the study, Mr. Fontenot arranged himself behind the desk, removing papers from his briefcase with practiced efficiency. Camille sat opposite him, feeling oddly like a schoolgirl called to the principal's office.

"Now then," the notary began, adjusting his spectacles. "The Last Will and Testament of Marie-Claire DuPont is quite straightforward in terms of material possessions. The estate of Le Vert Manor, including all buildings, land, and contents thereof, passes to you as her sole living descendant."

He pushed a document across the desk for her signature. Camille scanned it briefly before signing—standard legal language transferring ownership.

"Additionally, there are financial arrangements," Mr. Fontenot continued. "A trust account has been maintained for the property's upkeep—taxes, repairs, Eloise's salary. Modest but sufficient, provided the estate remains in family hands."

"And if I were to sell?" Camille asked.

Mr. Fontenot's eyebrows raised slightly. "That would be... problematic. The DuPont land is entailed with certain restrictions. Dating back to 1868, I believe. The property cannot be sold outside the bloodline."

"That can't be legal in modern times," Camille protested.

"You'd be surprised what holds legal weight in Louisiana parish law, especially with property this old." He removed his glasses, polishing them with a handkerchief. "But there is more to your inheritance than mere property, Miss DuPont."

From his briefcase, he withdrew a smaller envelope sealed with dark wax. "Your grandmother instructed me to deliver this personally, along with a verbal message."

"What message?"

"'The key is not merely metal.'" Mr. Fontenot recited, clearly not understanding the significance himself. "Does that hold meaning for you?"

Camille thought of the iron keys on the desk, particularly the one labeled "B" for basement. "Perhaps."

Thunder cracked outside, closer now. Rain began to patter against the windows as Mr. Fontenot gathered his papers.

"The deed transfer will be registered by week's end. The property taxes are paid through the year." He snapped his briefcase closed. "Is there anything else you require of me, Miss DuPont?"

A dozen questions crowded Camille's mind, none of which a parish notary could answer. "No, thank you."

After showing Mr. Fontenot out, Camille returned to the study. The storm had darkened the sky to twilight, though it was barely afternoon. Lightning flashed, briefly illuminating the grounds where the previous night's funeral had taken place.

She broke the seal on the envelope Mr. Fontenot had given her. Inside was a single page covered in what appeared to be a family tree. Names and dates stretched back to the 1860s, beginning with Josephine DuPont. Each generation showed multiple children, but only one female name in each was circled in red ink—the line of succession, Camille realized. Her own name appeared at the bottom, the only entry in her generation.

Beneath the family tree was a short note in her grandmother's hand:

The seventh daughter of the seventh line. The circle closes with you, Camille. The room holds the truth of our burden, but entering is accepting. Choose carefully.

A crash from upstairs interrupted her thoughts. Something heavy had fallen—or been thrown. Camille froze, listening. The house creaked and groaned around her, but no further disturbance came.

She glanced at the ring of keys still lying on the desk. The small one labeled "B" seemed to pulse with significance. The letter had mentioned a basement room, forbidden since childhood. Her grandmother's notes suggested it contained answers.

But first, she needed to check on the noise upstairs.

Camille ascended the staircase slowly, aware of every creak in the old wood. The upstairs hallway stretched in both directions, lined with closed doors. A flash of lightning illuminated the corridor, casting strange shadows that seemed to writhe along the walls.

"Hello?" she called. "Is anyone here?"

Only the rumble of thunder answered.

She moved toward her grandmother's suite at the end of the hall, where the sound had seemed to originate. The double doors were closed but unlocked. Steeling herself, Camille pushed them open.

The suite was exactly as she remembered from childhood—a sitting room opening to a large bedroom beyond. Her grandmother's possessions were arranged with precision, everything in its place. Nothing seemed disturbed.

Until Camille noticed the armoire. One of its heavy wooden doors hung open, and clothing spilled out onto the floor as if someone had been frantically searching through it. As she approached, the scent hit her—the same herbal, earthy smell that had permeated the funeral, now emanating from the scattered clothing.

Kneeling, Camille examined a garment—a white dress with intricate embroidery around the neck and sleeves. Hidden in its folds were small pouches sewn into the seams, each containing herbs and what looked like tiny bones.

A gris-gris. Camille recognized it from her childhood education about local traditions—a voodoo charm for protection.

Every garment in the armoire, she discovered, contained similar hidden pouches. Her grandmother had literally worn protection against supernatural forces every day of her life.

As Camille replaced the clothing, something caught her eye at the back of the armoire—a carved panel that didn't quite match the rest of the wood. She pressed it, and with a soft click, the panel swung inward, revealing a hidden compartment.

Inside was a leather-bound ledger much larger than the journal she'd found in her room. Camille pulled it out, along with a small wooden box beside it.

The ledger contained detailed records spanning decades. Each entry followed the same format: a date, a list of ingredients or components, a description of a ritual, and its intended purpose. Many included crude drawings of symbols—vevés—that Camille recognized from the funeral.

One entry from 1997 caught her eye:

August 17—Bound C. to the guardian spirit. Used her hair, my blood, graveyard dirt. She is too young to understand but not too young to be marked. The Baron was pleased with the offering. Seven years of protection guaranteed.

Camille—she had been eight years old in August 1997. The memory of standing beside the well with her grandmother returned sharply. She'd thought they were playing a game, drawing pictures in the dirt. Now she wondered what kind of "binding" had been performed on her without her knowledge.

The small wooden box contained vials of powders, bundles of dried herbs, and small bones wrapped in red cloth. Ritual components, she assumed, for whatever ceremonies her grandmother had been conducting.

A low rumble of thunder shook the house, and the lights flickered. Camille replaced everything except the ledger, which she tucked under her arm. The basement room beckoned—perhaps there she would find the full truth of what her grandmother had been doing all these years, and what she was now expected to continue.

Descending the stairs, ledger clutched to her chest, Camille felt a strange duality—part of her rational mind insisted this was all superstition and coincidence, while another part, deeper and more instinctive, recognized the truth in what she was discovering.

She retrieved the keys from the study and located the door to the basement—a heavy oak barrier beneath the main staircase that she had indeed been forbidden to approach as a child. The smallest key, labeled "B," fit perfectly into the iron lock.

As the key turned, Camille felt a subtle shift in the air pressure, as if the house itself had drawn a breath. The door swung inward, revealing stone steps descending into darkness.

A light switch by the door illuminated a single bare bulb at the bottom of the stairs. The weak yellow light barely penetrated the gloom, but it was enough to guide her descent.

The basement was larger than she expected, with rough stone walls and a packed earth floor. Old furniture and discarded household items crowded the space, draped in dusty sheets. But at the far end stood another door—newer than the rest of the house, made of metal with strange symbols etched into its surface.

This, then, was the forbidden room.

The key labeled "B" fit this lock as well. Camille hesitated, remembering her grandmother's warning: *"To enter is to acknowledge your role."* Was she ready to accept whatever legacy awaited her?

Lightning flashed from the small basement windows, briefly turning the room stark white. In that flash, Camille could have sworn she saw figures moving among the shrouded furniture—tall, thin shapes that weren't there when darkness returned.

Her heart racing, she made her decision. The key turned, and the metal door swung open with a groan.

Unlike the cluttered basement, the room beyond was meticulously organized. Shelves lined the walls, holding jars of preserved specimens, bundles of herbs, and books bound in materials Camille didn't want to identify. A large table dominated the center, its surface covered in a black cloth embroidered with silver symbols.

But what drew Camille's attention was the altar against the far wall.

Standing nearly six feet tall, it appeared to be a shrine to a single entity. A top hat rested on a wooden stand, surrounded by bottles of rum, cigars, and what looked disturbingly like human bones. Candles in black holders flanked the display, their wicks burned but currently unlit.

Baron Samedi. The loa of death in voodoo tradition. Camille recognized the imagery from her childhood in Louisiana, though she had never seen a shrine so elaborate—or so unsettling.

Beneath the altar was a drawer. Pulling it open, Camille found a leather-bound book much older than the ledger she carried. Its pages were brittle with age, the handwriting inside formal and antique—Josephine DuPont's journal, dated 1868.

The Baron has accepted my terms. Seven generations of service in exchange for prosperity and protection. Each daughter must maintain the binding or face the consequences of breaking faith. The veils between worlds must be maintained, lest what lies beyond break through entirely.

Beside the journal was a wooden box containing locks of hair tied with thread, each labeled with a name—every DuPont daughter in the direct line, including a small envelope marked "Camille, 1997."

The last item in the drawer made Camille's blood run cold—a list of names written in what appeared to be blood, now brown with age. Seven names, ending with her own. Beside each name except hers was a small symbol—the mark of completion. Her name alone remained unmarked.

A sound behind her made Camille spin around. The basement door had closed, though she didn't remember hearing it swing shut. She was alone in the forbidden room, surrounded by the evidence of seven generations of voodoo practice.

As if responding to her presence, the candles on the altar suddenly flared to life, though nothing had touched them. In their light, the hat seemed to tilt slightly, as though an invisible head beneath it had turned to observe her.

"Welcome home, daughter of the seventh line," a voice said from the darkest corner of the room.

Camille whirled toward the sound. Eloise stood there, though Camille hadn't heard her enter. The housekeeper's appearance had changed subtly—her back straighter, her eyes somehow darker and deeper.

"Your grandmother hoped you would never have to take up this burden," Eloise said, moving toward the altar. "She maintained the barriers longer than any before her, hoping to spare you. But time cannot be cheated forever."

"What is all this?" Camille gestured at the shrine, the books, the ritual implements. "What am I expected to do?"

"Continue what began in 1868. Maintain the barriers between worlds. Keep the loa satisfied with offerings so they do not seek more... substantial payment."

"This is insane," Camille whispered, though the candles burning with no apparent cause gave lie to her denial. "Voodoo isn't real. Spirits don't—"

"Tell that to the Breaux family," Eloise interrupted sharply. "Three cattle found this morning with their hearts removed, no blood spilled, no incisions visible. Tell that to the child who woke speaking in tongues last week, or the fisherman who pulled up his nets full of human teeth instead of shrimp."

She stepped closer, her face grave in the candlelight. "The barriers are failing. What your grandmother held at bay is pushing through. Without the proper rituals, without a DuPont daughter to maintain the pact, the loa will collect what they believe they are owed. And Baron Samedi does not accept substitutions."

Lightning flashed again, and in its glare, Eloise's face seemed to shift—for just an instant, resembling the eyeless wooden face of a ritual mask. When darkness returned, she was herself again, but Camille couldn't unsee the momentary transformation.

"What are you?" she asked, backing against the altar.

"A guide. The Laveau line has served this purpose since the beginning." Eloise's voice had taken on a rhythmic quality, almost hypnotic. "Your grandmother knew what was coming. She prepared as best she could. The signs are appearing faster now—the marked animals, the strange phenomena in town. Soon, the loa will seek human vessels. They are already testing the boundaries, looking for ways through."

"The figure in the cemetery," Camille said, remembering the woman with no mouth. "Was that—"

"A manifestation. A message." Eloise nodded. "The loa communicate through signs and symbols. That particular spirit is trying to warn you."

"Of what?"

"Of what happens when the Baron claims his due."

Another crash of thunder, and the lights went out entirely. Only the altar candles remained, casting wild shadows across the walls. In their flickering light, Camille could have sworn the specimens in jars turned to watch her.

"I can't do this," she said, clutching the ledger tighter. "I'm not a believer. I don't know the first thing about voodoo or spirits or—"

"Belief is irrelevant," Eloise cut in. "Blood is what matters. Blood began this pact, and only blood can maintain it... or end it."

"End it? My grandmother's letter mentioned breaking the pact entirely."

"At terrible cost." Eloise's expression darkened. "To break faith with the loa after seven generations of service would require a sacrifice greater than any your family has made before. The backlash would not be contained to just the DuPont line."

The implications settled heavily on Camille. Whatever she decided would affect not just herself but potentially the entire town.

"I need time to think," she said finally.

"Time is the one thing in short supply." Eloise gestured to the altar. "But yes, consider carefully. The room is yours now. The tools of your inheritance await your decision."

She turned to leave, then paused. "One more thing your grandmother would want you to know. The cloth doll—your guardian—it contains a portion of your spirit, bound when you were a child. Keep it close. It offers some protection while you decide."

With that, Eloise departed, leaving Camille alone in the candlelit shrine room.

For a long moment, she simply stood there, absorbing the enormity of what had been revealed. Seven generations of DuPont women had maintained a pact with voodoo spirits, performing rituals to keep supernatural forces at bay. Now that responsibility had fallen to her—a New York journalist who had spent her adult life dismissing such beliefs as superstition.

And yet... the candles still burned with no apparent fuel. The storm outside seemed focused precisely on Le Vert Manor. And the face of Eloise had shifted, however briefly, into something inhuman.

Camille gathered the journal, the box of hair locks, and the list of names. Whatever decision she made, she needed to understand fully what she was accepting—or rejecting.

As she turned to leave, the hat on the altar tilted further, as if its invisible wearer were bidding her farewell. A soft chuckle seemed to emanate from empty air, following Camille up the stairs and lingering in her mind long after she had locked the metal door behind her.

Outside, the storm raged on, lightning illuminating the swamp beyond the property where dark shapes moved among the cypress trees—too large to be animals, too fluid to be human.

Chapter 3
The Marked

---※---

Dawn broke reluctantly over Belle Noire, pale light struggling through clouds that had lingered after the night's storm. Camille sat in the kitchen, surrounded by her grandmother's journals, ledgers, and ritual notes, having spent most of the night attempting to make sense of the DuPont legacy.

The cloth doll sat on the table before her, its stitched face as expressionless as ever. According to what she'd read, the doll contained a portion of her spirit—a "soul jar" of sorts, bound when she was too young to remember or consent. The knowledge should have horrified her, but instead she felt a strange connection to the crude object, as if recognizing a part of herself.

"Did you sleep at all?" Eloise asked, entering with a basket of fresh herbs from the garden. The housekeeper looked perfectly normal in the morning light—no hint of the otherworldly transformation Camille thought she had glimpsed the previous evening.

"Not much," Camille admitted, rubbing eyes gritty from reading by candlelight. The electricity had returned shortly before dawn, but she'd been too engrossed to notice. "There's so much to understand."

"Understanding comes with time." Eloise began brewing coffee, the rich aroma filling the kitchen. "What matters now is acknowledging."

"I haven't decided yet," Camille said. "This is... it's a lot."

"The signs will continue, becoming more difficult to ignore." Eloise set a cup of coffee before her. "The loa grow impatient."

Camille sipped the hot coffee, gathering her thoughts. "Eloise, if my grandmother was maintaining these 'barriers,' as you call them, why did she let me leave? Why encourage me to go to New York, to build a life away from here?"

"Protection," Eloise replied simply. "Distance offered some safety. Your grandmother hoped that if she could maintain the pact long enough, the obligation might skip your generation entirely."

"Skip to whom? I have no children."

"That is part of the problem." Eloise busied herself chopping herbs. "The seventh generation was meant to complete the circle, to either fulfill the pact permanently or... face the consequences of breaking it."

"And my mother? Why did she leave?"

"Amelie saw too much, too young." A shadow crossed Eloise's face. "There was an incident when she was sixteen. A ritual gone wrong. After that, she wanted nothing to do with the family legacy. When she became pregnant with you, she fled completely."

"What kind of incident?"

Eloise hesitated. "A possession. A local boy—they were... close. He became a vessel for something that should not have crossed over. Your grandmother contained it, but not before Amelie witnessed things no child should see."

The implication hung in the air. Camille's mother had never spoken of Belle Noire or her own childhood, deflecting questions with vague references to "old superstitions" she had left behind.

"And now it's happening again," Camille said. "These 'signs' you mentioned—the cattle, the strange occurrences in town."

"Yes. But faster this time, more aggressive. The barriers weaken with each passing day."

Camille ran a finger along the worn cover of Josephine's journal. "What happens if I refuse this inheritance? If I just... leave?"

"The pact would be broken." Eloise's voice dropped to nearly a whisper. "Seven generations of protection would collapse. The loa would claim their due—not just from the DuPont line, but from all of Belle Noire. Blood debts do not simply vanish, Miss Camille."

Before Camille could respond, a knock at the back door interrupted them. Eloise answered it, admitting a young woman Camille didn't recognize—perhaps thirty, with worry etched on her face.

"Tante Eloise," the woman said, glancing nervously at Camille. "Can you come? It's Micah. He's... he's not right this morning."

"What's happened?" Eloise asked, already reaching for her shawl.

"He woke up speaking nonsense. Drawing things on the walls. His eyes..." The woman faltered. "They don't look like his eyes anymore."

Eloise exchanged a significant look with Camille. "It's beginning. Children are always the first to be affected."

"We should go," Camille found herself saying, surprising both Eloise and herself. "I want to see."

The woman—who introduced herself as Desiree Laveau, a cousin of Eloise's—led them to a small house at the edge of town.

Inside, family members gathered anxiously around a closed door, from behind which came a child's voice singing in what sounded like Creole, though the melody was discordant, unsettling.

"He's been like this since sunrise," Desiree explained. "Won't let anyone in the room. Locked it somehow, though there's no lock on that door."

Eloise approached the door, resting her palm against the wood. "Micah? It's Tante Eloise. Will you let me in, child?"

The singing stopped abruptly. A small voice answered—a child's tone but with an adult's cadence: "The seventh has returned. Does she bring completion or destruction?"

Eloise glanced back at Camille, who stepped forward hesitantly.

"Micah? My name is Camille. Can we talk?" she called through the door.

A scratching sound came from the other side, as if small fingernails were being dragged across the wood. "Not Micah now. Micah sleeps. We speak through him until the veils part fully."

"We?" Camille whispered to Eloise.

"The loa," Eloise murmured. "They've found a temporary vessel."

To the door, she said, "We mean no harm to Micah or to you. May we enter?"

Silence, then the distinct sound of a lock turning—though Desiree had been right, the door had no physical lock. It swung open slowly to reveal a small bedroom transformed.

Every surface—walls, ceiling, even the floor—was covered in crude drawings. Symbols Camille recognized from her grandmother's journals, rendered in what appeared to be black marker and, in some places, what might have been blood. In the center of the floor sat a boy of perhaps eight, surrounded by a circle of toy cars arranged in a perfect spiral.

But it was his eyes that seized Camille's attention—completely black, no whites visible, like pools of ink had replaced his irises.

"The seventh daughter comes at last," the boy said, his small face splitting into a too-wide grin. "Does she honor the pact or break it? Time grows short. The Baron's patience wanes."

"Who am I speaking to?" Camille asked, fighting to keep her voice steady.

The boy—or whatever spoke through him—tilted his head at an unnatural angle. "We are many, but today we are Legba. The keeper of crossroads. The opener of ways."

Eloise knelt just outside the spiral of toys. "We honor your presence, Papa Legba, but the vessel you've chosen is innocent. He cannot withstand your energy for long."

"All vessels are temporary until the veils fall," the boy replied. His gaze fixed on Camille. "You carry the mark already. The guardian spirit chose you long ago."

"The doll," Camille said, realization dawning. "That's what it means to be 'marked.'"

"The first binding." The boy nodded. "But incomplete. The Baron requires the seventh completion to honor the original pact."

"And if I refuse?"

The boy's expression darkened, and he began to tremble slightly, sweat beading on his forehead. "Then what was held at bay will come forth fully. The barriers that remain will collapse. Belle Noire will become a crossroads between worlds. The living will envy the dead."

His eyes rolled back suddenly, and he slumped forward. Eloise rushed to catch him before he hit the floor, the spiral of toys scattering.

"Micah!" Desiree cried, pushing past Camille to reach her son.

The boy's eyes fluttered open—normal brown eyes now, confused and frightened. "Mama? Why am I on the floor? Who drew on my walls?"

While Desiree comforted her son, Eloise examined the drawings covering the room. She touched one symbol, her expression grim.

"Warnings," she said quietly to Camille. "Prophecies. The barriers are thinning faster than I feared."

Camille studied the crude drawings. Many resembled the vevés from her grandmother's journals, but distorted, as if seen through warped glass. One recurring image caught her attention—a woman surrounded by snakes and flames, her hands raised toward a split sky.

"What does this mean?" she asked, pointing to the image.

"It is you," Eloise replied. "Or rather, what you must become. The final keeper—or the one who ends it all."

They left the Laveau house after ensuring Micah showed no lasting effects from his possession. The boy remembered nothing of the incident, and Eloise had mixed a tea for him that she promised would prevent further episodes—temporarily, at least.

Walking back toward Le Vert Manor, Camille struggled to process what she had witnessed. The rational explanations she had clung to were crumbling in the face of a child with black eyes speaking in a voice not his own.

"It's real, isn't it?" she said finally. "All of it. The spirits, the pact, everything."

"Yes," Eloise answered simply. "Your grandmother hoped you would never have to face this truth, but it seems the loa had other plans."

They passed through the town square, where a small group of children played near the ancient oak that served as Belle Noire's centerpiece. One child—a girl of perhaps six—broke away from the group and ran toward them, clutching a piece of paper.

"For you," the girl said, thrusting the paper at Camille. "The lady with no mouth told me to draw it."

Camille accepted the crude drawing, her blood running cold. A child's rendering of a woman surrounded by snakes and fire—nearly identical to the image in Micah's room. At the woman's feet was a distinct shape: a cloth doll with X's for eyes.

"Who is the lady with no mouth?" Camille asked gently.

"She comes at night," the girl replied matter-of-factly. "She tries to talk but can't. She's sad because she warned the others but they didn't listen."

"Warned them about what?"

"About the man in the top hat. He's hungry now." The girl looked past Camille toward Le Vert Manor in the distance. "She says you need to decide soon."

Before Camille could question her further, the girl's mother called her away, shooting suspicious glances at Camille and Eloise.

"The town knows something is happening," Eloise observed as they continued walking. "They can feel it, even if they don't understand it. Your grandmother's funeral stirred what was already awakening."

Back at Le Vert, Camille retreated to the study with the child's drawing and her grandmother's journals. The pieces were falling into place—a bargain made by Josephine DuPont in 1868, a pact with voodoo spirits that had sustained the family and protected the town for seven generations. Each DuPont daughter had maintained the barriers between worlds through ritual and sacrifice. Now the obligation had fallen to her.

As evening approached, Camille realized she hadn't eaten since morning. She made her way to the kitchen, only to stop short at the threshold. Muddy footprints crossed the floor, leading from the back door to the basement entrance—small prints, like those of a child, but strangely misshapen.

"Eloise?" she called, but received no answer. The housekeeper had mentioned errands in town after they'd returned.

Following the footprints cautiously, Camille found the basement door ajar, though she clearly remembered locking it. The muddy trail continued down the stairs. Heart pounding, she descended into the gloom.

The main basement area was undisturbed, but the metal door to the ritual room stood wide open. Inside, candles burned on the altar just as they had the night before. The shrine to Baron Samedi seemed to have shifted slightly, the hat angled differently, the bottles of rum rearranged.

Movement caught her eye—a shadow detaching itself from the corner, taking form as it approached.

It was the woman from the cemetery—tall and thin, wearing a white dress now stained with swamp mud. Her face was exactly as Camille remembered: smooth skin where her mouth should be, as if it had been erased entirely.

Instinctively, Camille reached for the wooden medallion she still wore around her neck. The mouthless woman stopped, making gestures with her hands—trying to communicate.

"Who are you?" Camille asked, her voice barely above a whisper.

The woman pointed to herself, then to the list of DuPont names still lying on the altar table. Specifically, she indicated the name just before Marie-Claire: Josephine DuPont II, who would have been Camille's great-grandmother.

"You're... a DuPont?" Camille guessed.

The woman nodded, then made a slicing motion across her own neck.

"You died," Camille interpreted. "But why are you... like this? What happened to your mouth?"

The woman turned toward the shrine to Baron Samedi, her posture conveying clear warning. She mimed drinking from a bottle, then clutched her throat in a pantomime of choking.

"Poison?" Camille guessed. "You were poisoned?"

The woman shook her head, frustrated. She pointed to the Baron's hat, then to herself, then made a sewing motion across her lips.

Understanding dawned. "The Baron took your voice. Because you tried to warn someone?"

An emphatic nod. The woman approached the altar and picked up a piece of chalk used for drawing ritual circles. On the stone wall, she wrote in shaky letters: HE LIES.

"Baron Samedi? The pact is a lie?" Camille asked.

More writing: NOT PROTECTION. PREPARATION.

"Preparation for what?"

Instead of answering, the woman dropped the chalk and grasped Camille's wrists. Her touch was ice-cold, her fingers like brittle twigs. Images flooded Camille's mind—Belle Noire transformed into a nightmarish landscape, buildings warped by impossible forces, people with black eyes like Micah's wandering the streets. Above it all, a massive figure in a top hat and tails, laughing as reality itself bent around him.

Camille wrenched away, gasping. "That's what will happen if I break the pact?"

The woman shook her head vehemently. She wrote again: IF YOU COMPLETE IT.

"That can't be right," Camille protested. "Eloise said—"

At the mention of Eloise, the woman's expression changed to one of alarm. She scribbled frantically: NOT WHAT SHE SEEMS. LAVEAU SERVES BARON.

Before Camille could respond, footsteps sounded on the basement stairs. The woman faded into shadow, her final message half-written on the wall: FIND THE TRUE—

"Miss Camille?" Eloise's voice called from the main basement. "Are you down here?"

Camille quickly smudged the chalk writing with her sleeve, heart racing. "Yes, just... checking something."

Eloise appeared in the doorway, carrying a basket of what looked like fresh herbs and candles. If she noticed the muddy footprints or the disturbed altar, she gave no sign.

"I've brought supplies," she said, setting down the basket. "The new moon is tomorrow night. If you've decided to accept your role, we should prepare for the first ritual of acknowledgment."

"I'm still... considering," Camille replied, trying to keep her voice steady. The warning from the mouthless woman—presumably her great-grandmother's spirit—had shaken her deeply. Who was telling the truth?

"Of course." Eloise nodded, arranging items on a shelf. "But you should know, three more cattle were found this morning on the Thibodeaux farm. And old Mrs. Guidry woke to find all the mirrors in her house shattered. The manifestations are increasing."

"And performing this ritual would help?"

"It would signal your acceptance of the mantle. The loa would know the pact continues." Eloise turned to face her fully. "Your grandmother prepared everything you need. The ritual itself is simple—an offering of blood to renew the DuPont commitment."

"Blood?"

"Just a few drops, willingly given." Eloise's expression softened. "I know this is overwhelming, Miss Camille. But your family has carried this burden for generations. It is your birthright, whether you embrace it or not."

Camille nodded absently, her mind racing. If her spectral great-grandmother was to be believed, completing the "Rite of Seven Veils" that her grandmother's letter had mentioned would bring disaster rather than prevent it. But Eloise—and apparently seven generations of DuPont women—believed they were protecting Belle Noire from supernatural forces.

"I need to clear my head," she said. "I'm going for a walk."

"Be back before dark," Eloise cautioned. "It's not safe to be outside after sunset, not anymore."

Camille climbed the basement stairs feeling the weight of Eloise's gaze on her back. Outside, the late afternoon sun cast long shadows across the grounds. On impulse, she headed toward the family cemetery where her grandmother had been buried just two days earlier—though it felt like weeks had passed since her arrival in Belle Noire.

The wrought iron gate creaked as she pushed it open. Her grandmother's grave was still fresh, the earth mounded and bare of grass. Camille knelt beside it, tracing the name etched in the temporary marker.

"What were you really doing all these years, Grandmère?" she whispered. "Protecting us or preparing something terrible?"

Only the whisper of wind through the cypress trees answered, carrying the earthy scent of the swamp and something else—a faint trace of tobacco and rum that reminded her of the Baron's shrine.

A movement among the graves caught her attention. A small green snake slithered across her grandmother's burial mound, its scales gleaming in the late afternoon sun. Camille wasn't normally afraid of snakes, but something about this one made her skin prickle—it moved with too much purpose, its eyes seeming to fix on her with intelligence beyond that of a simple reptile.

As she watched, frozen, the snake coiled itself into a spiral atop the grave. Then, impossibly, it began to stand upright on its tail, rising until its head was level with Camille's kneeling form. It opened its mouth, and a voice that was decidedly not that of a snake emerged.

"The seventh seeks truth," it hissed in a voice that sounded disturbingly like her grandmother's. "But truth has many faces."

Camille scrambled backward, nearly falling over another headstone. "What are you?"

"A messenger," the snake replied. "The loa speak through many vessels. The child. The woman without a mouth. Now this humble servant." It inclined its head toward the grave. "She who sleeps here sent me."

"My grandmother?" Camille's heart pounded. "Are you saying she's... controlling you somehow?"

"The dead walk close to the loa," the snake said cryptically. "She has a message: 'Trust no one completely. Not the Laveau woman. Not the spirits who speak through vessels. Not even me. Find your own truth, Camille. The final veil reveals all.'"

"What is the final veil?" Camille asked, her journalistic instinct for questioning overriding her fear. "What am I supposed to do?"

The snake began to lower itself, its body coiling once more upon the grave. "The ritual room holds the key to the seven veils. Each must be lifted in sequence. But beware—once begun, the path must be completed, one way or another."

"Or what happens?"

"Madness," the snake hissed, its body beginning to relax into a more natural position. "Possession. Dissolution of the self." Its eyes, briefly glowing with an unnatural light, began to dull. "Choose quickly, daughter of the seventh line. The Baron's patience wears thin. When next the moon hides her face, he will come himself to claim what is owed."

With that, the snake slithered away into the undergrowth, leaving Camille alone in the gathering dusk.

She rose shakily to her feet, brushing dirt from her knees. The sun hovered just above the treeline now, painting the cemetery in shades of gold and amber. Time to return to the house, if Eloise's warning about nightfall was to be believed.

As Camille turned to leave, she noticed something gleaming at the base of her grandmother's headstone—something that hadn't been there before the snake's appearance. She knelt again and found a small key of tarnished silver, intricate symbols etched along its shaft.

She pocketed it and hurried back toward Le Vert Manor, the shadows lengthening around her. The windows of the house glowed with warm light, a deceptively comforting sight given what she now knew lurked within its walls.

Eloise was waiting in the foyer, a small frown creasing her forehead. "You were gone longer than expected. Were you at the cemetery?"

"Yes," Camille admitted, seeing no reason to lie. "I needed to think."

"And have you reached a decision?"

"Not yet. But I'm getting closer." Camille headed for the stairs, the silver key heavy in her pocket. "I'd like to rest before dinner. It's been a long day."

"Of course." Eloise hesitated. "Miss Camille... perhaps you should sleep in your grandmother's room tonight. She had certain... protections in place there. Given how quickly things are progressing, it might be safer."

"I'll be fine in my own room, thank you." Camille didn't trust herself to elaborate without revealing her growing suspicions about Eloise's role in all this.

Upstairs, she locked her bedroom door and emptied her pockets, examining the silver key more closely. Its head was shaped like a stylized eye, and the symbols along its shaft resembled those from her grandmother's journals—vevés and sigils of protection or warding.

On a hunch, she retrieved the cloth doll from where she'd left it on her dresser. Turning it over, she discovered a tiny keyhole in its back, hidden beneath a flap of cloth. The silver key fit perfectly.

When she turned it, the doll's cloth body split open along a previously invisible seam. Inside was a folded piece of paper and a small glass vial containing what appeared to be blood.

The note, in her grandmother's handwriting, was brief:

Camille,

If you're reading this, you've begun to see beyond the veils. The Laveau woman serves two masters—our family, yes, but the Baron first. What she tells you is only partial truth.

The Seven Veils ritual is real. It must be completed before the new moon. But not as Eloise will instruct you.

My blood in this vial is the key to the true ritual. When the time comes, you will know how to use it.

Trust the guardian spirit. She cannot speak, but she guides true.

The Baron's hunger must be satisfied, but not with what he thinks he's owed.

—M.C.D.

Camille stared at the note, then at the vial of blood—her grandmother's blood, preserved for this moment. The conflicting messages were making her head spin. Eloise claimed one thing, the mouthless woman (apparently a guardian spirit) warned of another, and now her grandmother's posthumous message suggested a third path.

What was clear: something had to be done before the new moon, now just one day away. The Seven Veils ritual was key, but not necessarily in the way Eloise described.

A soft thud from downstairs interrupted her thoughts. Voices drifted up—Eloise speaking to someone at the front door. Camille cracked her door open to listen.

"—spreading faster than we anticipated," a man's voice was saying—Mr. Thibodeaux, she thought. "The Landry child is showing signs now too. Eyes gone black, speaking in tongues."

"The seventh hasn't fully committed yet," Eloise replied, her voice tight with concern. "We may need to... encourage her decision."

"How? The Baron was specific—it must be willingly done."

"There are ways to shape willingness." Something in Eloise's tone sent a chill through Camille. "Bring the child here tomorrow at sunset. Perhaps seeing another vessel will... clarify things for Miss Camille."

The conversation continued, but their voices moved deeper into the house, becoming unintelligible. Camille closed her door silently, mind racing. Were they planning to use a possessed child to manipulate her? And what did Eloise mean by "shaping willingness"?

Night had fallen completely now, the darkness outside her window absolute. Camille realized she'd missed dinner, but hunger was the least of her concerns. She needed to understand the Seven Veils ritual before tomorrow's new moon, and it seemed the basement room held those answers.

But venturing there now, with Eloise and Mr. Thibodeaux somewhere below, discussing plans that apparently involved her cooperation... it was too risky. She would need to wait until the house was quiet.

Camille spread her grandmother's journals across the bed, searching for references to the ritual. Most entries were frustratingly vague, speaking of "maintaining the barriers" and "feeding the loa" without specific instructions. But one passage, dated just three months ago, caught her attention:

The seventh veil grows thin. I feel him testing the barriers nightly now. The other six hold, but barely. Camille must return soon. Only the seventh daughter can complete the circle or break it entirely. I've prepared both paths, though I pray she chooses wisely.

The true ritual waits in the hidden place. The false one is what they expect.

The hidden place. Not the basement room, which Eloise knew intimately, but somewhere else. Somewhere only a DuPont would know to look.

Camille's gaze fell on the cloth doll, its stuffing visible through the open seam where she'd extracted the note and vial. On impulse, she turned it over and examined the stitching more carefully. X's for eyes, a simple line for a mouth, but on the back of its head, nearly invisible unless you were looking for it, was a tiny symbol embroidered in thread barely darker than the doll itself.

She recognized it from the cemetery—the same symbol had been carved into the base of every DuPont headstone. A family sigil of sorts.

Where else had she seen it? The manor had been so full of symbols and carvings, it was hard to recall a specific one. Then it came to her: the well. The old well in the backyard, where her grandmother had performed the "first binding" according to the photo she'd found. Its stone rim was carved with symbols, and she was certain the family sigil was among them.

A plan formed in her mind. She would wait until the house was silent, then investigate the well. If her instincts were correct, it might hold the "hidden place" her grandmother had mentioned— and the true ritual for the Seven Veils.

Hours passed as Camille pored over the journals, piecing together fragments of information. The grandfather clock in the hallway struck midnight, and still she heard occasional movements downstairs. Eloise seemed to be having a restless night as well.

Finally, around one in the morning, the house fell silent. Camille changed into dark clothing, tucked the vial of blood and the silver key into her pocket, and cautiously opened her door.

The hallway was dark except for slivers of moonlight through the windows at each end. She crept downstairs, avoiding the steps she remembered creaking from childhood. The foyer was empty, the parlor door closed. A thin line of light showed beneath Eloise's quarters off the kitchen—the housekeeper was still awake.

Moving silently, Camille slipped out the side door onto the verandah. The night air was thick with humidity, the chirping of insects providing cover for any sound she might make. The moon, just a sliver away from new, provided little illumination, but Camille knew the path to the well by heart.

It stood in what had once been a formal garden, now overgrown with native plants reclaiming their territory. The well itself was ancient—predating the house, according to family lore. Built of stacked stone and topped with a wrought iron frame for the pulley, it had been dry for generations, its depths a source of childhood fascination and fear.

As she approached, Camille noticed fresh markings in the dirt surrounding the well—a perfect circle drawn around its perimeter, intersected by straight lines forming a seven-pointed star. At each point of the star, a small object had been placed: a feather, a stone, a bone, a coin, a dried flower, a lock of hair, and—most disturbingly—what appeared to be a small, severed finger, withered with age.

The ritual preparations had already begun, it seemed. But by whose design—Eloise's or her grandmother's?

Camille stepped carefully over the lines in the dirt, approaching the well's stone rim. In the faint moonlight, she ran her fingers over the carved symbols until she found it—the DuPont family sigil, a stylized fleur-de-lis intertwined with what might have been a snake.

She pressed it, remembering how the panel in her grandmother's armoire had responded to similar pressure. Nothing happened. She tried turning it, pushing from different angles. Still nothing.

The silver key. On impulse, she withdrew it from her pocket and examined the well rim more carefully. There, beside the sigil, was a small hole that might accept a key. She inserted it, holding her breath.

The key turned smoothly, and a section of the stone rim shifted with a faint grinding sound. A hidden compartment was revealed, containing a small metal box. Camille extracted it carefully, heart pounding with anticipation and fear.

Inside the box lay a leather-bound booklet, much smaller than the journals she'd been reading, and a cloth bag that clinked with the sound of glass vials. The booklet's cover bore a single title: "The Seventh Veil."

A twig snapped behind her. Camille whirled, clutching the box to her chest.

Eloise stood at the edge of the ritual circle, her expression unreadable in the darkness. "I wondered when you'd find it," she said quietly. "She always said you were clever, just like Josephine."

"How long have you been watching me?" Camille demanded, trying to keep her voice steady.

"Long enough." Eloise took a step forward but remained outside the circle. "You should have come to me, Camille. The ritual is dangerous without proper guidance."

"Whose guidance? Yours or my grandmother's?" Camille held up the booklet. "Because it seems she left very specific instructions that don't require your interpretation."

Eloise sighed, a sound of genuine weariness. "Marie-Claire was a visionary, but she grew... confused in her final years. What she believed would save Belle Noire might instead destroy it."

"Or perhaps it's the other way around." Camille stood her ground, the well at her back. "The guardian spirit warned me. So did my grandmother, in her own way. What's the real purpose of the Seven Veils ritual, Eloise? What happens in the seventh generation?"

A long silence stretched between them. Finally, Eloise spoke, her voice different somehow—deeper, with a rhythmic cadence Camille hadn't heard before.

"The veil between worlds thins completely. What was separated becomes joined again. The loa walk freely once more." She took another step forward. "It has been the plan since Josephine first made the pact—not to keep the spirits out, but to prepare the way for their return."

"And the people of Belle Noire? What happens to them?"

"Some become vessels. Some serve. Some feed the hunger of spirits too long denied their rightful place in this world." Eloise's eyes seemed to gleam in the darkness. "The Baron has waited patiently through seven generations of DuPont women, each maintaining just enough separation to prevent total crossing, each preparing the ground for what comes next. You are the culmination, Camille. The Opener of Ways."

"And if I refuse? If I break the pact instead?"

"Then what began with blood must end with blood. Yours, specifically." Eloise's posture had changed, becoming unnaturally still. "The Baron does not relinquish claims easily. If the seventh veil is not opened properly, he will tear through regardless, taking you as his entry price."

Understanding dawned, cold and terrible. "That's what happened to my great-grandmother, isn't it? She refused to complete the ritual, tried to warn others."

"Josephine II." Eloise nodded. "She discovered the truth too soon, before preparations were complete. She tried to perform a counter-ritual, to seal the veils permanently rather than open them. The Baron took her voice first, then her life. Her blood strengthened the sixth veil, but the seventh remained."

"Waiting for me." Camille clutched the box tighter. "But I'm not doing it. I'm not opening the way for your Baron or any other spirit to possess the people of this town."

"It's not possession, Camille. It's elevation. Transcendence." Eloise's voice had taken on an evangelical fervor. "Humans and loa joined as they were always meant to be. The Baron has promised power to those who serve willingly."

"And you believe him? After what happened to my great-grandmother?"

"I am Laveau. My family has served the loa faithfully for centuries. We will be rewarded." Eloise finally stepped over the ritual line, entering the circle. "Now, give me the box. The true ritual must not be performed."

"Stay back." Camille edged sideways, keeping the well between them. "I don't want to hurt you, Eloise."

A sound like dry laughter emerged from the housekeeper's throat—a sound Camille was certain no human could make. "Hurt me? Child, you have no idea what I am."

Eloise's face seemed to shift in the moonlight, features becoming sharper, more angular. Her movements as she circled the well were too fluid, almost serpentine.

"You're possessed," Camille realized aloud. "The loa are already using you as a vessel."

"Not possessed. Blessed." Eloise—or whatever spoke through her—reached out with fingers that seemed unnaturally elongated. "Now give me the box, and I'll ensure your passing is painless. Fight, and the Baron will take you piece by piece, as he did your great-grandmother."

Camille feinted left, then darted right, making a break for the edge of the circle. Eloise moved with inhuman speed, cutting off her escape. They circled each other around the well, predator and prey in a deadly dance.

"You cannot leave the circle now that you've entered it," Eloise said. "Not until the ritual is complete—one way or another."

Camille's mind raced. The circle, the seven-pointed star—they formed a ritual space, a place between worlds where the veils were already thinning. If she couldn't escape...

The well. The hidden place.

Without hesitation, Camille swung herself over the stone rim and onto the narrow ledge inside. Below yawned absolute darkness—the well shaft descending into the earth.

"Foolish girl!" Eloise hissed, lunging for her. "There's no escape that way, only a long fall and broken bones."

But Camille had spotted something Eloise couldn't see from her angle—iron rungs embedded in the well wall, forming a ladder into the darkness. She tucked the box into her shirt, grasped the first rung, and began to descend.

Eloise's face appeared above her, contorted with rage. Hands reached down, grasping at air as Camille descended beyond her reach.

"The Baron will find you!" Eloise's voice echoed down the shaft. "There is nowhere in Belle Noire he cannot reach!"

Camille continued climbing down, rung by rung, into the stygian darkness. The air grew cooler, then warmer again in a way that defied natural physics. The sounds from above faded, replaced by a soft humming that seemed to emanate from the walls themselves.

How long she climbed, she couldn't tell. The well shaft should have been perhaps thirty feet at most, but she had been descending for what felt like minutes, the ladder extending far beyond what should have been possible.

Finally, her foot touched solid ground. The humming was louder here, rhythmic and almost musical. Camille fumbled in her pocket for her phone, activating its flashlight.

The beam revealed a small circular chamber at the bottom of the well, its walls lined with the same symbols she had seen throughout Le Vert Manor. At the center stood a stone altar, its surface carved into the shape of a seven-pointed star identical to the one Eloise had drawn above.

This was it—the hidden place her grandmother had prepared, beyond Eloise's reach. Camille approached the altar, setting the metal box upon it. As she did, seven niches in the wall around the chamber illuminated with soft blue light, revealing seven veils of translucent fabric hanging like curtains across small alcoves.

The Ritual of Seven Veils. Not metaphorical at all, but an actual physical ritual her grandmother had prepared in secret.

With trembling hands, Camille opened the booklet from the box. Her grandmother's handwriting filled the pages, describing a ritual very different from what Eloise had implied above.

The Seven Veils separate worlds that should remain distinct. Each veil, when lifted properly, strengthens the barrier rather than weakens it. This is the truth the Baron has kept hidden—the ritual he demands is designed to tear down the veils, but performed correctly, it will seal them permanently.

My blood carries the power of six generations of binding. When mixed with yours—the seventh—it creates the final seal. Each veil must be lifted in sequence, each alcove faced directly.

But be warned: behind each veil waits a trial. The loa will test your resolve with visions, with fear, with temptation. Succeed, and the barriers strengthen. Fail, and all is lost.

Camille opened the cloth bag, finding seven small vials arranged in numbered order, each containing a different substance. Following her grandmother's instructions, she placed the first vial—containing what appeared to be graveyard dirt—on the altar.

As soon as it touched the stone, the first veil began to ripple as if caught in an unfelt breeze. Steeling herself, Camille approached it. The moment her fingertips touched the fabric, the world dissolved around her.

Chapter 4
The Binding

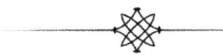

Camille found herself standing in Belle Noire, but not as she knew it. The town sprawled before her as it might have appeared in the 1860s—the buildings newly constructed, the streets lined with carriages instead of cars. People in period clothing moved about their business, oblivious to her presence.

A woman in an elegant burgundy dress walked directly toward her—Josephine DuPont, Camille recognized from portraits. Her great-great-grandmother, founder of the DuPont legacy in Belle Noire.

"You see now," Josephine said, stopping before her. "The beginning."

"This is... a vision?" Camille asked, looking around in wonder. The scene felt solid, real in every sensory detail—the smell of horses, the sound of conversation, the heat of the Louisiana sun.

"Memory," Josephine corrected. "Blood remembers, even across generations."

She gestured, and the scene shifted. They stood now in what Camille recognized as the parlor of Le Vert Manor, though newer, grander. Josephine—the real Josephine, not the spectral guide beside Camille—knelt on the floor, surrounded by candles and strange symbols drawn in what appeared to be blood.

A tall figure stood before her—a man in an impeccable black suit and top hat, his face painted half white like a skull. Baron Samedi, manifested fully.

"The first pact," the spectral Josephine explained. "The War had left us destitute. Union soldiers occupied our land. I sought power to restore what was lost."

The Baron's voice filled the room, though his painted lips barely moved: "Seven generations. Seven veils between worlds. Each daughter will maintain the barrier, keeping the way prepared but not yet open. In the seventh generation, the final choice—to open fully or close forever."

"And what do you offer in return?" the kneeling Josephine asked.

"Prosperity. Protection. Power over those who would destroy you." The Baron smiled, a terrible sight on his half-skull face. "The Yankees will abandon your lands. Your fortunes will return. Your enemies will fall before you."

"And the price?"

"Blood. A little each month to maintain the veils. And when the seventh generation comes, a final offering." The Baron's gaze seemed to penetrate time itself, fixing on Camille. "Her choice will determine all."

The scene shifted again. Now they stood in the cemetery, watching as generation after generation of DuPont women performed rituals at the graves of their predecessors. Blood dripped onto the earth, symbols were drawn, prayers and incantations offered.

"Each of us maintained the barriers," Josephine explained. "Not understanding the Baron's true purpose."

"Which was?" Camille asked, though she suspected the answer.

"To prepare Belle Noire as a gateway. A place where the veil between worlds is so thin that, with one final ritual, it could be torn open entirely." Josephine's expression hardened. "The loa wish to walk the physical world again, to take human vessels, to feed on human essence. They have been denied this for centuries, their worship diminished, their power contained."

The vision flickered, showing brief, terrifying glimpses of what might follow such an event—Belle Noire transformed into a nightmarish landscape, its inhabitants possessed by entities never meant to walk the human world.

"My daughter realized too late," Josephine continued as the vision shifted to show her daughter performing a similar ritual. "As did hers. Each believed they were protecting the town, not preparing it for consumption."

"Until my great-grandmother," Camille said, remembering the mouthless woman.

"Josephine II discovered the truth." The spectral Josephine nodded. "She attempted to alter the ritual, to seal the veils permanently rather than maintain them as the Baron instructed. For her defiance, he took her voice, then her life."

"And my grandmother? She knew the truth too?"

"Marie-Claire learned from her mother's fate. She pretended compliance while secretly developing the true ritual—the one you have begun." Josephine gestured around them. "Seven veils, seven trials. Face each truth, accept the burden of knowledge, and use my blood—our blood—to seal the barriers forever."

The vision wavered, reality bleeding through at the edges. Josephine's form began to fade.

"Wait!" Camille called. "What do I need to do exactly?"

"Face each veil," Josephine's voice echoed as she disappeared. "Accept the truth it shows. Mix your blood with ours at the final veil. Complete the circle or break it forever. But beware—the

Baron knows you are here. He will try to stop you, to twist the ritual to his purpose."

With that, Camille was thrust back into the well chamber, gasping as if she'd been underwater. The first veil had fallen, revealing an empty alcove. On the altar, the first vial had turned to dust.

Six more to go, and time was running short. Above, she could hear Eloise calling her name, the sound distorted as if coming through water. The housekeeper couldn't reach her here, but dawn would eventually come, and with it the new moon. The ritual needed to be completed before then.

Camille placed the second vial on the altar—this one containing what looked like crushed herbs and bone fragments. As before, the corresponding veil began to ripple. She approached and touched it, bracing herself for another vision.

This time, she found herself in a hospital room, watching her mother in the final stages of cancer. Amelie DuPont had withered to almost nothing, her once-beautiful face gaunt and gray. Beside the bed sat Marie-Claire—Camille's grandmother—looking much as she had when Camille last saw her alive.

"You could save her," a voice whispered from the shadows. "The loa have power over life and death. A simple offering, and her illness would vanish."

Camille recognized the speaker without seeing him—Baron Samedi, lord of the dead. His presence filled the hospital room like smoke.

"At what cost?" Marie-Claire asked, her voice steady despite her obvious grief.

"The usual. Blood. Devotion. Perhaps a small sacrifice from the girl." The Baron's attention shifted to a corner where a teenage

Camille dozed in an uncomfortable chair. "Nothing she would miss terribly. A finger, perhaps. Or an eye."

"No." Marie-Claire's refusal was absolute. "We have maintained the pact as agreed. You will not have my granddaughter."

"Then your daughter dies," the Baron said simply. "Tonight. In pain."

Marie-Claire closed her eyes briefly, then opened them with renewed resolve. "So be it."

The scene shifted. Now Camille stood invisible beside her younger self at her mother's funeral. Marie-Claire approached, placing a hand on teenage Camille's shoulder.

"You must leave Belle Noire," she said quietly. "Go north. Build a life far from here."

"Because of what took Mom?" Young Camille asked, tears streaming down her face.

"Yes. But also because of what awaits here." Marie-Claire glanced around as if checking for eavesdroppers. "I will hold the barriers as long as I can. Perhaps long enough that you never need to return."

"I don't understand," Young Camille said.

"Better that way, for now." Marie-Claire pressed something into her hand—the cloth doll Camille now knew contained a portion of her own spirit. "Keep this with you. It will ward off certain influences, give me time to find another way."

The vision blurred, then reformed to show Marie-Claire in the basement room, performing complex rituals while Eloise watched from the doorway, her expression calculating.

"She suspects," the spectral voice of Josephine commented, though Camille couldn't see her. "The Laveau woman serves the Baron willingly. She knows Marie-Claire seeks a way to break the pact."

"Then why let her observe the rituals?" Camille asked the empty air.

"To allay suspicion. To buy time." The disembodied voice was growing fainter. "The true work happened here, beneath the well, where Laveau blood cannot follow."

The scene shifted one final time, showing Marie-Claire in the well chamber, much as it appeared now. She was older, frailer, working quickly to prepare the seven alcoves, the seven vials.

"My strength fades," she murmured to herself. "The cancer spreads. The Baron thinks it natural decay, but I know better. He influences cells as easily as minds."

She placed the final vial—the one containing her blood—into the cloth bag.

"Camille must finish what I cannot. The seventh veil will be her trial alone."

With that, the vision faded, returning Camille to the well chamber. The second veil had fallen, revealing another empty alcove. On the altar, the second vial had turned to dust.

Two down, five to go. Camille checked her phone—barely an hour had passed, though the visions had seemed to last much longer. Still, dawn approached, and with it, the new moon. She needed to work quickly.

The third vial contained what appeared to be water, though it moved strangely within the glass, almost as if alive. Camille placed it on the altar with growing confidence, watching as the third veil began to stir.

This vision was different—no spectral guide, no historical scenes. Instead, Camille found herself alone in the swamps surrounding Belle Noire, darkness pressing in from all sides. The moon above was new, providing no light. Yet somehow, she could see.

Movement in the water caught her attention. Something large was circling, displacing the still surface of the swamp. Not an alligator—something much larger, its shape indistinct but somehow wrong.

"The third veil shows what lurks beyond," a voice whispered—not Josephine's, not the Baron's, but something older, more primal. "The hunger that waits for the gateway to open."

The thing in the water rose slightly, revealing a glistening surface that might have been scales or might have been something else entirely. Eyes—too many eyes—blinked open along its length, fixing on Camille with ancient malevolence.

"We remember when humans were prey," the voice continued, emanating from the creature itself. "We remember the taste of mortal fear. Seven generations we have waited, watching through the thinning veils."

More movement around her—shapes rising from the muck, from behind cypress trees, from the very air itself. Entities never meant to walk the human world, held at bay by the barriers her family had maintained, however unwittingly.

"The Baron is but our herald," the first creature said, beginning to emerge further from the water. "Our negotiator in the world of men. But we are the ones who hunger. We are the ones who will feed when the veils fall."

Camille stood her ground despite the primal terror rising within her. "And if I complete the ritual? If I seal the barriers permanently?"

A sound like laughter rippled across the swamp, disturbing the water in concentric circles. "Then we wait. Time means little to us. Another bargain will be struck, another family bound. The hunger is patient, but it is also eternal."

The creature lunged suddenly, jaws opening impossibly wide to reveal row upon row of needle-like teeth. Camille flinched but didn't run—remembering her grandmother's instructions. Face each truth. Accept the burden of knowledge.

"I see you," she said, forcing herself to look directly at the monstrosity before her. "I acknowledge your hunger. But I deny you satisfaction."

The creature froze mid-lunge, suspended in the air mere inches from her face. Its many eyes blinked in what might have been surprise.

"Brave," it hissed. "Like the one before you. But she grew old. She weakened. You will too, eventually."

"Maybe," Camille admitted. "But tonight, the veils will be sealed. Find your feast elsewhere."

The swamp scene dissolved around her, the creature's frustrated howl following Camille back to the well chamber. The third veil had fallen, the third vial turned to dust.

Moving faster now, she placed the fourth vial on the altar—this one filled with what looked like quicksilver, though it moved with an intelligence that no metal should possess. The fourth veil rippled, and Camille stepped forward to touch it.

This vision struck more personally. Camille found herself in her New York apartment, surrounded by the trappings of her successful life—awards for her journalism, photographs with celebrities and politicians, evidence of the career she had built far from Belle Noire.

A knock at the door revealed a version of herself—a doppelgänger perfect in every detail except for the eyes, which were completely black, like Micah's had been during his possession.

"You could have this back," her double said, gesturing to the apartment. "The Baron is generous to those who serve willingly. Your life in New York, your career, all of it—with the added power of his patronage."

The doppelgänger moved through the apartment, trailing fingers across Camille's possessions. "Think of the stories you could write with access to both worlds. The insights no other journalist could claim. You would be legendary."

Camille watched as her double picked up a prestigious journalism award. "This? A trinket compared to what you could achieve with the Baron's blessing."

"At what cost?" Camille asked, already knowing the answer.

"Belle Noire, of course." The doppelgänger shrugged. "The town was always meant to be a gateway. Those with the right bloodlines will be vessels, those without... sustenance."

Camille looked around at her New York apartment, the trappings of success she'd worked so hard to achieve. For a moment, the temptation was real—to accept the Baron's deal, to return to her life with enhanced power and insight, to leave Belle Noire to its fate.

"They're strangers to you now," her double continued, voice honeyed with persuasion. "You left them behind years ago. What do their lives matter compared to your potential?"

Camille thought of Micah, the possessed child with black eyes. Of the other townsfolk who, despite their suspicions and fear of her family, were innocent in this generational bargain.

"No," she said firmly. "I reject your offer."

Her double's face contorted with rage, the human mask slipping to reveal something ancient and terrible beneath. "Then you will lose everything—your life here, your future, perhaps your very soul."

"So be it," Camille replied, surprised by her own resolve.

The vision shattered, fragments of her New York life falling away like broken glass. Camille found herself back in the well chamber, the fourth veil fallen, the fourth vial dust.

She worked quickly now, aware of a growing pressure in the air, as if the chamber itself were breathing. The fifth vial contained what looked like tiny fragments of bone suspended in oil. As soon as she placed it on the altar, the fifth veil began to undulate violently, as if something behind it were trying to break through.

Steeling herself, Camille touched the fabric.

This vision was different—not the past or a temptation, but a possible future. Belle Noire transformed, its buildings warped by forces never meant to exist in the physical world. The sky above hung low and bruised, pulsing with unnatural colors. Townsfolk wandered the streets, their eyes solid black, their movements jerky and uncoordinated, as if their bodies were ill-fitting costumes worn by entities unused to human limitations.

In the town square, a massive figure presided over the scene—Baron Samedi, now twenty feet tall, his top hat scraping the diseased sky. Beside him stood Eloise, transformed into something no longer entirely human, her limbs elongated, her face a ritual mask come to life.

And there, among the Baron's inner circle, was another version of Camille—not the New York professional from the previous vision, but something else. This Camille wore ceremonial robes emblazoned with voodoo symbols. The cloth doll that contained part of her spirit hung from her belt, now transformed into something grotesque, its stuffing replaced with writhing shadows.

"The seventh daughter who completed the circle," a voice whispered. "The one who opened the way."

The Baron turned his skeletal face toward the real Camille, somehow perceiving her presence in this vision of what might be. His laughter boomed across the twisted landscape.

"Still fighting the inevitable?" he asked, voice like grinding stones. "This is the destiny your ancestors prepared for seven generations. The veils will fall, with your willing participation or without it."

"You lied to them," Camille accused. "To all of them, from Josephine onward."

"I merely allowed them to believe what they wished." The Baron spread his massive hands. "They wanted prosperity, protection. I provided both, asking only for small sacrifices. Blood, devotion, the occasional ritual." His grin widened impossibly. "That the rituals were preparing Belle Noire as a gateway was... an omission, not a lie."

The Baron gestured, and the vision expanded to show more of the transformed town. Behind the warped buildings, creatures moved—things with too many limbs, too many eyes, forms that seemed to bend reality around them.

"My associates grow impatient," the Baron continued. "Seven generations they have waited while I prepared the way. The hunger builds."

The vision-Camille stepped forward, her eyes now solid black like the other possessed townsfolk. "You can't stop this," she told the real Camille. "Better to join willingly, to maintain some semblance of self, than to be taken by force."

Camille looked from her corrupted self to the Baron, to the monstrosities lurking at the edges of the transformed Belle Noire. Despite her fear, she felt her resolve hardening.

"My grandmother found another way," she said. "A way to seal the veils permanently."

The Baron's laughter cut off abruptly. "Marie-Claire tried and failed. As did Josephine II before her." His voice dropped to a dangerous whisper. "Would you like to see what became of your great-grandmother when she defied me?"

The scene shifted, showing a woman Camille recognized from photographs—Josephine II, her great-grandmother. She stood in the basement ritual room, surrounded by protective symbols hastily drawn in various substances. Before her, a younger Baron Samedi materialized, his expression cold with fury.

"The pact cannot be broken," he told her. "Seven generations. Seven veils. Such was the agreement."

"The agreement was based on lies," Josephine II replied, her voice steady despite her obvious fear. "I will not prepare this town for slaughter."

"Then you will serve as an example." The Baron moved with inhuman speed, his fingers elongating into talons that seized Josephine's face. "First, your voice—so no warnings may be given."

Camille forced herself to watch as the Baron's magic sealed her great-grandmother's mouth, leaving only smooth skin where lips had been. Josephine II's silent scream was visible only in her eyes, wide with agony.

"Then, your life—to strengthen the sixth veil," the Baron continued, driving those same talons into Josephine's chest. "Your daughter will learn from your mistake. She will maintain the barriers properly, preparing for the seventh generation."

The vision blurred, then refocused to show the Baron turning toward Camille again. "Your grandmother was more subtle in her defiance, but no more successful. The cancer that took her? My gift, for her attempted betrayal."

"Yet here I am," Camille replied, finding strength in her anger. "Completing the ritual she prepared."

"A futile gesture." The Baron waved dismissively. "You lack her knowledge, her experience. Even she could not break the pact entirely—only delay it."

"We'll see." Camille focused on the vision of Belle Noire transformed, committing its horrors to memory. "I accept this possibility. I acknowledge the danger. But I reject its inevitability."

The Baron's face contorted with rage, but before he could respond, the vision shattered. Camille found herself back in the well chamber, gasping for breath. The fifth veil had fallen, the fifth vial turned to dust.

Two more to go. The chamber trembled slightly, dust falling from the ceiling. The pressure in the air had increased, making it difficult to breathe. Above, Camille could hear distant shouting—Eloise, perhaps, or something worse.

The sixth vial contained what appeared to be blood—darker than human blood should be, almost black in the chamber's dim light. This, Camille realized, must be her great-grandmother's blood, taken when the Baron killed her.

With reverent care, she placed the vial on the altar. The sixth veil convulsed violently, as if something powerful were trapped behind it, desperate to break free.

This vision was immediate and overwhelming—Camille found herself experiencing her great-grandmother's final moments from within, feeling Josephine II's terror and resolve as if they were her own.

She/Josephine stood in the basement ritual room, surrounded by protective symbols. She had discovered the truth about the Baron's plan and had begun developing a counter-ritual—one that would permanently seal the veils rather than prepare them for opening.

The Baron's arrival, his fury, his punishment—Camille felt it all as Josephine had. The agony of having her voice stolen, her mouth sealed. The terror of knowing she would die without warning her daughter. The despair of failing to protect Belle Noire.

But beneath the fear and pain, Josephine II had maintained a final, desperate hope. As the Baron's talons pierced her chest, she had focused her dying thoughts on a single purpose: infusing her blood with a power the Baron didn't anticipate—the power to close the seventh veil permanently.

Her last thought, which Camille now experienced as her own: *The seventh daughter will finish what I began. Blood calls to blood across generations.*

The vision ended abruptly as Josephine II died, but Camille remained connected to her great-grandmother's consciousness for a moment longer—long enough to understand what she had done. With her dying breath, Josephine II had transformed her blood into a key—one that, when combined with the blood of the seventh generation, could lock the veils forever.

Camille returned to herself in the well chamber, tears streaming down her face. The sixth veil had fallen, the sixth vial turned to dust. Only one remained—her grandmother's blood, preserved in the vial she had found inside the cloth doll.

Before she could place it on the altar, a violent tremor shook the chamber. Dust and small stones rained from the ceiling. From above came a sound like tearing fabric—massive and world-altering—and with it, a voice that seemed to fill all available space.

"ENOUGH!" Baron Samedi's voice thundered through the well shaft. "The game ends now, daughter of the seventh line!"

The wooden ladder leading up the well burst into splinters. The ritual chamber's walls began to crack, supernatural pressure building from outside. The Baron was coming—or trying to.

Camille fumbled in her pocket for her grandmother's vial of blood. The final test, the seventh veil, still awaited her. But would she have time to complete it before the Baron broke through?

The ceiling fractured, a jagged line spreading across the stone. Through the widening gap, Camille glimpsed a night sky that couldn't possibly exist—stars in impossible colors, constellations that hurt the eyes to look upon. The veil between worlds was thinning dangerously.

With trembling hands, she placed the seventh vial—her grandmother's blood—on the altar. The final veil began to glow, pulsing with a light that seemed to come from somewhere beyond physical reality.

This was it—the culmination of seven generations of DuPont women, of sacrifice and manipulation and resistance. Whatever lay behind that seventh veil would determine whether Belle Noire became a gateway for hungry entities or remained protected from them forever.

Camille reached for the glowing fabric, bracing herself for whatever trial awaited her beyond.

Chapter 5
The Rite of Seven

Camille's fingers touched the glowing veil, and the world dissolved around her.

Unlike the previous visions, she found herself in a featureless void—no landscape, no structures, only formless light that shifted through colors she had no names for. She stood on nothing, surrounded by nothing, yet somehow remained upright.

"The seventh veil," a voice said—not the Baron's, not Josephine's, but her grandmother's. Marie-Claire DuPont materialized before her, looking healthier and younger than when Camille had last seen her alive. "The final barrier."

"Grandmère," Camille whispered, fighting the urge to embrace the apparition. "Is it really you?"

"In a way." Marie-Claire smiled sadly. "What remains of me after death. Enough to guide you through this final trial."

"The Baron is breaking through," Camille said urgently. "The chamber is collapsing."

"Time moves differently here, between the veils. We have what we need." Marie-Claire gestured, and the void around them transformed into a perfect recreation of the basement ritual room. "This is where it ends—or begins anew."

The spectral Marie-Claire moved to a cabinet Camille hadn't noticed before. From it, she withdrew seven objects: a feather, a stone, a bone, a coin, a dried flower, a lock of hair, and a small silver knife.

"The seven elements of binding," she explained, arranging them in a circle. "Each representing a generation of DuPont women. Each carrying a portion of power accumulated over 150 years."

"What do I need to do?" Camille asked, eyeing the knife nervously.

"Complete the circle. Add your blood to mine—to all of ours." Marie-Claire indicated the center of the circle where a small, shallow bowl now sat. "But first, you must choose."

"Choose what?"

"Whether to seal the veils permanently or to open them fully." Marie-Claire's expression was grave. "Sealing them means cutting Belle Noire off from the loa forever—both the malevolent ones like the Baron and the benevolent spirits that have guided the town since its founding."

"And if I choose to open them?"

"The Baron has shown you that future." Marie-Claire shook her head. "A gateway between worlds, Belle Noire transformed into a feeding ground."

"Then there's no choice at all," Camille said firmly.

"There is always choice, Camille." Marie-Claire touched her granddaughter's cheek gently. "But there is also cost. Sealing the veils permanently will require more than a few drops of blood. It will demand a significant sacrifice."

"What kind of sacrifice?"

The spectral Marie-Claire hesitated. "A portion of yourself. Not your life—I would never ask that—but something nearly as precious. Your connection to your past, to who you are."

"My memories," Camille realized aloud.

"Yes. Not all of them—you would still be yourself, still know your name, your basic skills. But your connection to Belle Noire, to our family, to the events that have brought you here... those would be severed."

Camille considered this. To lose the traumatic events of the past few days wouldn't be so terrible. But to forget her grandmother, her childhood in Belle Noire, perhaps even her mother...

"There is no perfect solution," Marie-Claire continued softly. "The pact Josephine made was flawed from the beginning, built on deception. Breaking it comes at a cost."

Outside the vision, Camille could sense the physical world continuing to fracture. The Baron was getting closer to breaking through, the protective barriers of the well chamber crumbling.

"I'll do it," she said decisively. "Tell me how."

Marie-Claire's face showed both pride and sorrow. "Take the knife. Add your blood to the bowl where mine already waits. As you do, focus your will on sealing the veils permanently. The sacrifice will happen naturally—the magic will take what it needs."

Camille picked up the silver knife, its blade gleaming with an inner light that matched the glow of the seventh veil. She held her palm over the bowl, noting that it already contained a small amount of dark red liquid—her grandmother's blood.

"One last thing," Marie-Claire said as Camille prepared to cut. "The Baron will fight this with everything he has. When you feel him trying to pervert the ritual, to twist it to his purpose, remember that blood calls to blood. Our combined strength is greater than his."

With a deep breath, Camille drew the blade across her palm. Blood welled immediately, dripping into the bowl to mingle with her grandmother's. As the first drops touched, a sizzling sound filled the air, and the mixture began to glow with the same unearthly light as the seventh veil.

"Now focus," Marie-Claire instructed, her form beginning to fade. "Seal the veils. Close the gateway. End the pact."

Camille concentrated on her intent, visualizing barriers solidifying, pathways closing, walls strengthening between worlds. The mixture in the bowl pulsed in rhythm with her heartbeat, growing brighter with each passing second.

Suddenly, pain lanced through her head—an invasion, a foreign presence trying to seize control of the ritual. The Baron, fighting to turn her efforts to his advantage.

"Blood of my blood," a voice hissed in her mind, the Baron's voice twisted with rage and desperation. "Seven generations of preparation. You cannot undo it now!"

Camille felt her will wavering as the Baron's presence pressed against her consciousness. Images flashed before her eyes—Belle Noire consumed, her own body taken as a vessel, the Baron triumphant as the veils fell completely.

"Blood calls to blood," she gasped, remembering her grandmother's words. "Our combined strength is greater than yours."

Concentrating on the bloodline that connected her to six generations of DuPont women, Camille pushed back against the Baron's intrusion. She felt them responding—Josephine, her daughter, her granddaughter, all the way to Marie-Claire, and finally to herself. A chain of determination and resistance spanning over 150 years.

The bowl of mingled blood erupted with light so intense it should have blinded her. The seven objects surrounding it rose into the air, spinning in a circle that gradually tightened, drawing closer to the glowing mixture.

"No!" the Baron's voice roared, both in her mind and seemingly in the physical world beyond the vision. "The pact cannot be broken!"

"It already is," Camille replied, feeling power surge through her as the ritual neared completion.

The seven objects plunged simultaneously into the bowl of blood. A shockwave of energy exploded outward, throwing Camille backward. As she fell, she felt something tearing away from her—memories, connections, pieces of her identity flowing out like water from a broken vessel.

Her grandmother's face... fading. Belle Noire's streets... growing dim. Her mother's voice... silencing. Her own childhood... dissolving.

The Baron's scream of rage was the last thing Camille heard as darkness claimed her.

She awoke to the sensation of rain on her face. Opening her eyes, Camille found herself lying in mud beside a massive oak tree. Dawn was breaking, the first rays of sunlight piercing through storm clouds that were already beginning to disperse.

Sitting up gingerly, she surveyed her surroundings. She was in a cemetery—an old one, judging by the weathered headstones. Nearby stood a wrought-iron fence, and beyond it, the charred remains of what must have been a large house, still smoldering despite the rain.

Confusion clouded her mind. How had she gotten here? What was this place?

Looking down, she noticed her clothes were torn and muddy. Her palm bore a fresh cut, still seeping blood. Around her neck hung a wooden medallion carved with strange symbols she didn't recognize.

"Miss? Are you hurt?" A voice startled her.

A young girl stood at the cemetery gate, watching her with wary curiosity. "You were out here all night during the storm. Everyone's been looking for you."

"Looking for me?" Camille asked, her voice hoarse. "Why?"

The girl tilted her head, confused by the question. "Because of the fire at Le Vert Manor. They wanted to make sure nobody was inside."

The name meant nothing to Camille. "I don't... I'm not sure why I'm here."

"What's your name?" the girl asked.

A simple question, yet it sent panic rippling through Camille. "I'm..." She searched her fractured memories. "Camille. Camille DuPont."

The name felt right on her tongue, but evoked no further recollections. She knew she was Camille DuPont, knew she was from... somewhere else. New York? Yes, that felt correct. But why she was in this cemetery, in this town, remained a mystery.

"You should come with me," the girl said, extending her hand. "My mama can help you get cleaned up."

As Camille rose unsteadily to her feet, she noticed something half-buried in the mud beside her—a small cloth doll with X's for eyes and a simple line for a mouth. Without knowing why, she picked it up, brushing away the dirt with gentle fingers.

"That's a gris-gris doll," the girl observed. "For protection. My grandmere makes them."

Camille nodded as if she understood, though the term meant nothing to her. Still, the doll felt important somehow. She slipped it into her pocket.

Following the girl through the cemetery gate, Camille glanced back once at the still-smoldering ruins of the manor house. For a brief moment, she thought she saw a figure standing among the graves—a woman in white with no mouth, her hand raised in farewell.

Camille blinked, and the figure was gone. Just a trick of the light and the mist rising from the rain-soaked ground. Nothing more.

"What's the name of this town?" she asked the girl as they walked away from the cemetery.

"Belle Noire," the girl replied. "Don't you remember?"

"No," Camille said quietly. "I don't remember at all."

As they reached the main road, Camille noticed townsfolk emerging from their homes, pointing at the smoke still rising from the manor ruins. Their faces showed a strange mixture of fear and relief, as if the fire had been both a tragedy and a blessing.

Meanwhile, deep beneath what remained of Le Vert Manor, in a well shaft now collapsed and sealed, seven veils hung in a chamber that existed between worlds. Behind each veil, an empty alcove. On a stone altar, seven vials turned to dust. And etched into the altar's surface, a new symbol—one that had not been there before—the mark of a bargain completed, a circle closed, a pact both fulfilled and broken.

Belle Noire would continue, free from the Baron's influence, the gateway between worlds sealed permanently. The cost: one woman's connection to her past, to her family legacy, to the truth of what had happened.

As Camille walked toward the town with the girl, rain washing away the last traces of mud from her clothes, the cloth doll in her pocket seemed to pulse with a subtle warmth, like a heartbeat. A guardian spirit, watching over her still.

In her mind, whispers faded like the last echoes of a forgotten dream: *Blood calls to blood. The seventh veil is sealed. The binding is complete.*

Epilogue
Ashes and Salt

---※---

Three days later, Camille stood at the bus stop on the outskirts of Belle Noire, a single suitcase at her feet. The townspeople had been kind, providing clothes, shelter, and gentle questioning about who she was and how she'd come to be in the cemetery that night.

She had few answers to give them. Her name was Camille DuPont. She was from New York, where she worked as a journalist. She had no memory of coming to Belle Noire or why she might have been at the manor when it burned.

Doctor Broussard had examined her and found no physical cause for her memory loss—no concussion, no evidence of trauma beyond exhaustion and the unexplained cut on her palm, now healing nicely. "Sometimes the mind protects itself," he'd suggested gently. "Perhaps you witnessed something in that fire too terrible to remember."

The local sheriff had checked her identification, verified her employment at a New York magazine, and made arrangements for her return. "No reason to keep you here," he'd said, though Camille had noticed the relief in his eyes when she mentioned her plans to leave.

Now, waiting for the bus that would take her to New Orleans and then a flight back to New York, Camille tried once more to pierce the fog surrounding her recent past. She remembered her apartment, her colleagues, her life in the city. But everything related to Belle Noire remained a blank, despite the townsfolk's insistence that she had arrived just days before the fire, asking questions about her grandmother.

A grandmother she couldn't remember. A family connection to this town she couldn't feel.

The cloth doll sat in her jacket pocket, her one inexplicable attachment from her time here. She'd tried several times to leave it behind—on the dresser at Mrs. Thibodeaux's house where she'd been staying, or on the table at the local diner—but each time, she found herself retrieving it before she could walk away.

"You heading back to the big city?" Mr. Thibodeaux approached, interrupting her thoughts. He'd been kind enough to drive her to the bus stop, though their conversation during the ride had been stilted, as if he knew more than he was willing to share.

"Yes," Camille replied, offering a polite smile. "Thank you for all your help."

He nodded, shifting uncomfortably. "Listen, Miss DuPont... about your grandmother's property. The land, what's left of it after the fire..."

"The sheriff mentioned something about that. It belongs to me, apparently."

"It does. Been in your family for generations." He cleared his throat. "If you're not planning to return, there are folks in town who might be interested in purchasing it."

Camille considered this. The land meant nothing to her now—just a charred mansion and an overgrown estate she couldn't remember. "That seems reasonable. Have your lawyer contact mine in New York."

Relief washed over Mr. Thibodeaux's face. "Much obliged. Some folks thought you might want to rebuild, continue the family... tradition."

"What tradition is that?" Camille asked.

"Oh, just... DuPonts have always lived at Le Vert Manor, is all." He glanced at his watch. "Bus should be along any minute now."

As if on cue, the sound of an engine rumbled in the distance. Mr. Thibodeaux picked up Camille's suitcase, carrying it to the roadside where the bus would stop.

"One last thing," he said hesitantly. "That doll you've been carrying. It's a local type of charm. Protective, supposedly." He paused. "Might be best to leave it here. Some things don't... travel well beyond Belle Noire."

Camille's hand went instinctively to her pocket, feeling the doll's soft form. "I think I'll keep it. A souvenir."

Mr. Thibodeaux's expression tightened slightly, but he nodded. "Your choice, Miss DuPont. Always has been."

The bus rounded the corner, slowing as it approached the stop. Mr. Thibodeaux handed the suitcase to the driver, then turned to Camille with an extended hand.

"Safe travels. If you ever... remember anything about your time here, might be best to let it lie."

Camille shook his hand, noting the calluses and the slight tremor. "Why do you say that?"

"Some knowledge doesn't improve life none." He stepped back as the bus door opened. "Goodbye, Miss DuPont."

Boarding the bus, Camille found a window seat and watched as Belle Noire began to recede behind her. Strange how a place could feel simultaneously foreign and familiar, as if she were leaving somewhere important without knowing why.

As the bus passed the turn for the cemetery, Camille glimpsed a figure standing beneath the oak tree—a woman in white, watching the bus depart. For a second, their eyes seemed to meet across the distance, and Camille felt a jolt of recognition that faded as quickly as it had come.

She reached into her pocket, fingers closing around the cloth doll. Despite its crude construction, it felt precious somehow. Throughout her stay in Belle Noire, she'd experienced the oddest sensations while holding it—brief flashes of insight, fragments of what might have been memories, gone before she could grasp them fully.

The bus hit a pothole, jolting her from her thoughts. The doll slipped in her grip, and Camille felt something hard inside its stuffing. Curious, she probed gently with her fingers, feeling what seemed to be a small key hidden within the cloth body.

Part of her wanted to investigate further, to cut open the doll and discover what secrets it might hold. But another part—a stronger instinct she couldn't explain—warned against it. Some doors, once opened, couldn't be closed again.

Camille returned the doll to her pocket unopened, turning her gaze forward as Belle Noire disappeared around a bend in the road. Ahead lay New Orleans, then New York, then the life she remembered. Behind lay mysteries she couldn't recall and perhaps never should.

The wooden medallion still hung around her neck, hidden beneath her blouse. Like the doll, she couldn't bring herself to part with it, though she couldn't explain its significance. Sometimes at night, half-asleep, she thought she heard whispers emanating from both objects—names she almost recognized, warnings she almost understood.

In those moments between wakefulness and dreams, fragmented images sometimes surfaced: a basement room filled with candles, a well shaft descending impossibly deep, a skeletal figure in a top hat reaching for her with elongated fingers. But by morning, these visions faded, leaving only vague unease and the sense of having narrowly escaped something terrible.

As the bus continued its journey away from Belle Noire, Camille closed her eyes, allowing the rhythm of the road to lull her toward sleep. In her pocket, the cloth doll shifted slightly of its own accord, its stitched face turned upward as if watching over her. Around her neck, the wooden medallion warmed against her skin.

Far behind them, atop the ruins of Le Vert Manor, birds circled warily, refusing to land despite the promise of salvage. The locals would later say that nothing ever grew again on that blighted soil, that animals avoided the property entirely, that on certain nights when the moon was new, strange lights could be seen dancing in the cemetery where generations of DuPonts lay buried.

But Camille DuPont would not hear these stories. She would return to New York, resume her career, build a life unburdened by knowledge of family curses and generational pacts. Sometimes, in her dreams, she would hear a woman's voice warning her: "The seventh veil holds. The binding is complete. But nothing is forever."

And she would wake, reaching instinctively for the cloth doll that never left her nightstand, drawing comfort from its presence without understanding why.

In a cemetery in Belle Noire, seven headstones stood in a perfect arc, marking the resting places of seven generations of DuPont women. Before the most recent grave, freshly dug but now beginning to settle, a small depression remained in the earth—the exact size and shape of a cloth doll that had been removed and carried away.

The binding was complete. The veils were sealed.

For now.

Three months later, Camille sat at her desk in the New York magazine office, fingers hovering over her keyboard. Her editor had been patient with her return, understanding that trauma and memory loss required adjustment time. But now, deadlines loomed again, and the blank document before her seemed insurmountable.

The assignment was simple—a piece on urban legends and folklore in modern America. Once, she would have approached it with journalistic detachment, analyzing the psychological need for myths in contemporary society. Now, she found herself hesitating, uncertain why the topic filled her with unnameable dread.

Her hand drifted to the cloth doll perched beside her computer monitor. Against all professional decorum, she'd insisted on keeping it at her desk, ignoring colleagues' curious glances. Something about it anchored her when the world seemed to tilt sideways—moments that came with increasing frequency since her return from Louisiana.

"Still working with your little voodoo friend?" Markus, a fellow writer, leaned against her cubicle wall, nodding toward the doll.

"It's not voodoo," Camille replied automatically, then paused, wondering how she knew that with such certainty.

"Whatever you say." Markus shrugged. "Listen, I found something interesting for your folklore piece. An anthropology professor at Columbia specializes in Gulf Coast spiritual traditions. Thought you might want to interview her."

He placed a business card on her desk: "Dr. Josephine Laveau, Department of Anthropology."

The name struck Camille like a physical blow. Laveau. Something important about that name hovered just beyond recall.

"You okay?" Markus asked. "You went pale there."

"I'm fine," Camille managed. "Thanks for this."

After he left, she examined the card more closely. An unexpected compulsion seized her—she needed to meet this professor, though she couldn't articulate why.

Two days later, Camille sat in Dr. Laveau's office, recorder ready, notebook open. The professor was younger than she'd expected, perhaps early forties, with intelligent eyes that seemed to evaluate Camille with unusual intensity.

"Your article on folklore sounds fascinating," Dr. Laveau said, gesturing for Camille to sit. "Though I'm curious why you specifically wanted to discuss Louisiana traditions."

"I..." Camille hesitated. "I spent some time there recently. Belle Noire. But I don't remember much of it."

Dr. Laveau's casual demeanor shifted subtly. "Belle Noire? Interesting choice. Not many outsiders find their way there."

"I had family connections, apparently. The DuPonts."

At this, Dr. Laveau's expression changed entirely. She rose and closed her office door.

"Miss DuPont," she said quietly, returning to her seat. "I believe our meeting may not be coincidence. My grandmother was Eloise Laveau."

The name sent a shock through Camille's system—a flash of a kitchen, herbs being ground in a mortar, a woman with knowing eyes.

"I don't..." Camille began, but Dr. Laveau raised a hand.

"You wouldn't remember her. That was part of the sacrifice." She reached into her desk drawer, removing a small leather-bound book. "This arrived for me a week after the fire at Le Vert Manor, sent by my grandmother before she disappeared."

She slid the book across her desk. Camille hesitated before touching it, inexplicable anxiety tightening her chest.

"What is it?" she asked.

"A record. Of seven generations of DuPont women. Of a pact made and finally broken." Dr. Laveau studied Camille's face. "And of what was taken from you in exchange."

Camille's fingers trembled as she opened the book. Inside, in elegant handwriting she somehow recognized without knowing how, was a detailed account of the DuPont family's connection to voodoo spirits, to Baron Samedi, to the ritual of Seven Veils.

And on the final page, a message addressed to her:

Camille,

If you are reading this, the sacrifice was accepted. Your memories of Belle Noire, of our family's burden, of the ritual you completed—all taken as payment for sealing the veils permanently.

I could not guide you through the final trial. That journey was yours alone. But I can offer this: what was taken can sometimes be recovered, though never completely, never purely.

The cloth guardian contains what remains of your connection to Belle Noire. The key hidden within will unlock more than memory, should you choose to use it.

Some doors are better left closed. Some knowledge is better left forgotten. The choice, as always, is yours.

--Marie-Claire DuPont

Camille closed the book, a dull ache building behind her eyes. "Is this some kind of joke?"

"I assure you, it's not." Dr. Laveau's voice was gentle but firm. "My grandmother served your family for decades, maintaining the rituals that kept Belle Noire protected—or so she believed."

"But... voodoo spirits? Supernatural pacts? This is—"

"Unbelievable? Yes. Yet you carry a cloth doll you cannot part with, wear a wooden medallion that feels warm against your skin, and have dreams of a figure in a top hat calling your name."

Camille stared at her, shocked. "How could you know that?"

"Because they were predicted. Side effects of a ritual that changed reality itself." Dr. Laveau leaned forward. "My grandmother believed the Baron would return eventually. That sealing the veils was temporary, not permanent. She sent me this book to prepare for that day."

"Why tell me? If I sacrificed my memories to end this, why risk bringing it back?"

Dr. Laveau's expression softened. "Because you have a right to choose—to know or not know. And because three nights ago, in Belle Noire, a child woke speaking in tongues. Her eyes completely black."

The description triggered another memory flash—a boy surrounded by toys arranged in a spiral, his eyes like pools of ink.

"The signs are appearing again," Dr. Laveau continued. "Whatever you did, however powerful the ritual, the Baron is finding ways to test the barriers."

Camille's hand went to her pocket, feeling the outline of the cloth doll. "And the key? The one inside the doll?"

"I don't know exactly. My grandmother's notes suggest it opens something in Belle Noire—something that might restore what you lost."

"Or unleash what I contained," Camille finished, the words coming from somewhere beyond conscious thought.

She left Dr. Laveau's office with the book and more questions than answers. That night in her apartment, she removed the cloth doll from her pocket and examined it closely. The stitching along its back had loosened somehow, as if the doll itself were offering access to its secrets.

Carefully, Camille widened the opening. Inside, nestled among cotton stuffing now gray with age, was a small silver key ornately carved with symbols she almost recognized.

As her fingers closed around it, images flooded her mind—a well shaft descending impossibly deep, seven veils glowing with unearthly light, her own blood mingling with another's in a ritual bowl.

The wooden medallion around her neck grew hot against her skin. Outside her apartment window, a storm gathered unexpectedly, lightning illuminating the New York skyline in brief, violent flashes.

Camille stared at the key in her palm, feeling threads of memory beginning to reweave themselves into a pattern she wasn't sure she wanted to recognize. The sacrifice had been made, the veils sealed, Belle Noire saved—at the cost of her connection to her own past.

Now she had to choose again: pursue these fragments, possibly unraveling what she had sacrificed so much to achieve, or close this door firmly and permanently.

Behind her, a shadow stretched across her apartment wall—longer than it should have been, shaped like a man in a top hat. When she turned, nothing was there.

But in the back of her mind, barely audible, a voice like grinding stones whispered: "The seventh veil thins again, daughter of the final line. Our dance is not yet finished."

Camille clutched the key tighter, decision crystallizing. She would return to Belle Noire one last time—not to remember, but to ensure what she had forgotten remained safely sealed away.

In the gentle glow of her apartment lights, the cloth doll's stitched face seemed to smile for the first time since she'd found it in the mud beside her grandmother's grave. The guardian had delivered its message. The circle was preparing to turn again.

Outside, the storm intensified, rain lashing against her windows like impatient fingers demanding entry. Thunder boomed—or perhaps it was laughter, echoing from somewhere beyond the veil of ordinary reality.

THE END

Enjoyed this book?

Share your thoughts with a review and help more readers discover it! Your feedback truly makes a difference.

☆ ☆ ☆ ☆ ☆

To be the first to read my next book or for any suggestions about new translations, visit: https://arielsandersbooks.com/

SPECIAL BONUS

*Want this Bonus Ebook for **free**?*

SCAN W/ YOUR CAMERA TO DOWNLOAD THE EBOOK!

Printed in Dunstable, United Kingdom